ONCE UPON A LIFE

Roy

More than a friend.
In many ways more than
a brother.

Just a fellow crew-member
and a Kriegie — which means
the very best.

Dib

ONCE UPON A LIFE

Robert Dibben

The Book Guild Ltd
Sussex, England

The Book Guild Ltd
25 High Street,
Lewes, Sussex

First published 1994
© Robert Dibben
Set in Baskerville

Typesetting by
Formaprint Ltd,
Worthing, West Sussex

Printed in Great Britain by
Antony Rowe Ltd,
Chippenham, Wiltshire.

A catalogue record for this book is
available from the British Library

ISBN 0 86332 940 3

1

'As you know, Fergie, whilst in no way eccentric has recently become somewhat unconventional in thoughts expressed, deeds done and more importantly, duties left undone. A tentative suggestion I made to talk things over met with not much more than a shy grin. With one notable exception Fergie is his own person, a loner. So although his note asking, almost insisting that I meet with him in his room at six o'clock suggested alarming urgency, I was not unduly surprised or perturbed when he himself was not there at twelve minutes beyond that hour.

It was then that the corridor attendant looked in bearing a very welcome cup of what I thought and hoped would be tea.

'Mr Ferguson left the coffee in the cup already' she said. 'He asked me to make it for you if he was not back by ten past. I was to tell you that he was called away and, if not here on time, he should not be very long and would you wait'.

'Thank you Mrs Mason', I smiled towards her. 'Now off you go and goodnight.'

A sip or two of the coffee convinced me that I would have been better pleased had Fergie left a teabag instead.

It was still daylight but in the first shade of sundown the cone shaped desk lamp which had been on throughout, now cast a distinct circle of light upon an assortment of articles, usually to be found at the desk of a person carrying a heavy workload. I found myself attempting to read papers placed there, but from a reverse angle. When that task became laboriously difficult I slowly lost interest.

The circus was the same brilliant spectacle it had always been since the days of my childhood. The ring, a blaze of dazzling light effecting a blanket of darkness to all outside its perimeter. From my position, seemingly at a high point of the viewing arrangements, I could see four or more acts being performed simultaneously, suggesting a grand climax — maybe the end of the show.

I felt quite alone except for a voice over the tannoy repeatedly calling: 'Come along Mr Ferguson,' suggesting that Fergie was somewhere among the audience who were, strangely, quite silent. Equally strange to me was how I came to be present at the circus at all. However, any possible explanation for my presence seemed of little importance as my gaze was again drawn to the varied acts in progress. Two distinct sets of gymnasts were performing on the floor of the ring. One could only be amazed at the physical strength and nimble prowess necessary to accomplish the statuesque combinations achieved at what seemed to be the roll of a drum. Except there was no roll of a drum.

One team of six athletes had just reached what must surely have been the culmination of their act. A huge fellow standing, feet firmly placed on the ground, fully supported the other five. Four athletes hung out from his massive frame; one to the front, one to the rear and one on each side. The remaining lad, having placed his head to the special skull cap worn by the anchor man, was stretched erectly with toes pointing to heaven, his outspread arms being the only assistance to perfect balance.

On the edge of the ring, furthermost from my position, another team with equal skill and precision and with the aid of one large and one small springboard had just bounced themselves into a column of human flesh. With one man standing on the floor, three more were standing on the shoulders of the man below. This balancing feat, so high and so perfectly executed, brought to my mind the giant totem poles I had seen in Western Canada.

Some fifteen feet above their heads, trapeze artists clad in shining silver-tight costumes reflecting the brilliant lighting from on high, swung rhythmically, interchanging to a metronome-type beat to ensure precise handling. A veritable delight to the eye!

Toward the apex of the big top and, level with the eye line, was the undoubted star of the show. She was sitting — no lying, arched over the bar of the trapeze with legs outstretched, the soles of her feet pointing directly towards me. Her arms, shoulders and head, on the far side of the swing, hung back and down from the position of her bottom on the bar, describing an arc pointing towards the ground. Her outfit, a gun metal leotard with a cut away top revealing her back, shoulders, neck and face, produced a terrific contrast to the stunning lines of her marble white beauty; the golden tresses of her hair a crowning glory.

Awaiting, with some excitement, the commencement of her act, I was aware of the gutteral sound of the repeated message over the tannoy to Mr Ferguson. More than one Ferguson in the world, I supposed. Need not necessarily have involved our Fergie.

I became quite irritated, even agitated, as the voice continued and was aghast as my view of the circus began to break up, or rather melt down, before my eyes and the actual scene before me became a stark reality.

A muzzy head and hazy vision did not prevent the realisation that the illusions experienced whilst drugged, bore a positive relationship to articles on the desk before me: the ring and big top fantasy induced by the cone of light from the desk lamp; a pyramid of gymnasts had become quite another pyramid — a desk object used for the retention of all manner of rubber stamps, date, signature facsimile, department, document category and so on, as you well know; my human totem pole — no more exciting than a biro pen, upright in its desk stand. Close by, a stapler and staple remover, articles from which stupor had conjured a large and small springboard. And the delightful young stars of the trapeze? Simply chrome balls suspended on threads, forming the desk attraction which produces an illusion of perpetual motion. 'Newton's cradle', is that what it's called? A slight movement below the conical shade of the desk lamp caught my line of sight and I found myself looking at the lethal end of a .22 Barretta, the small model favoured by the ladies, either for show or in earnest. The aim line of the barrel seemed disturbingly close to the bridge of my nose. The gun was held in a gloved female hand, a grey glove, loose at the wrist with an open vent towards the palm of the hand. Just above the top a uniquely attractive bracelet, a broad band of link-weave gold, hung from a slender wrist. From that combination my bemused senses had fantasised a beautiful star of the show.

With my head now clearing I made to straighten up from the slouched position in which I occupied the chair, prompting the male voice into yet more action:

'So now Mr Ferguson it is time to talk, or rather for you to listen.'

Although bright the desk-top lamp did not reflect, or diffuse, sufficient light to illuminate beyond the immediate desk area. I peered towards the walls and corners but as the room was not my own I could not be sure if a bulky shadow indicated furniture or one of my visitors. The Barretta threat was no longer visible in the light of the lamp but gravel voice continued on and on. It was a most uninteresting and unpleasant monotone.

''You have failed to respond to communications or to attend confessional at appointed times'' he droned. 'Our success depends upon the strength of each and every link in the chain. The Cardinal has concerned himself with the performance of your duties. The knowledge you have acquired, if misused, could be a danger to our cause. If you are no longer with us you must be considered a threat. If you have not resumed your obligation prior to Tuesday of next week, that is five days hence, I am instructed to apply the conditional terms of your initiation.

'How is your dear friend, John, by the way?

'We shall leave now. Do be at the meeting on Tuesday. Not to be there will be viewed seriously, very seriously!'

The restricted light from the lamp, the position of the door and a well carpeted floor together with an inability to think clearly, contributed to a lack of awareness of movement or of presence within the room. A sound of light, hurried, scuffling footsteps coming from the corridor, however, had me struggling awkwardly from the chair. Using the desk lamp as a torch to sweep an area of light around the room I made for the door, switched on the ceiling lights and moved into the corridor as fast as my rubbery legs would allow. Normal lighting for that area was off, only the glow from low-powered amber bulbs at stretegic points remained. I got to the lift cage and its surrounding stair-well. With the lift not readily available I trundled down the stairs realising that I must be falling five or more seconds behind my quarry, in every ten of pursuit.

At ground floor level I headed for the main hall where a badminton match was in progress and, aware that neither players nor spectators would have eyes for anything or anyone else, I hurried on to the main doors leading to the Strand, almost shouting to the attendants there:

'Have you seen a man and a woman leaving within the past few moments?'

''Yes, the sergeant is checking them out from the car

park, right now.''

I moved as fast as I could to where the security sergeant was relocking the huge iron gates which lead from the West Green, also into the Strand. I repeated the question to which he replied:

"Yes, I have just let them out. Is there something wrong? They arrived about twenty-five minutes ago." And reading from the clip-board in his hand: "Here we are, 7.52, in a silver grey Montego, G468 GKN. I booked them in myself. Said they were visiting Mr Ferguson. I said I'd ring him but they were here by appointment. Offered to see them up but they knew the way. They had identification, Mr and Mrs Tulley. My, she was a cracker!''

He was just about the poorest example of a security officer that one could possibly imagine. The only act he successfully completed, with regard to the protection of the building, its personnel and its contents, was to lock the gate after they had left. Allowing the female caller, concealing a hand gun, to get as far as Fergie's room was deserving of more than a slap on the wrist. She obviously caught his eye but not for the reasons he had been placed at the check point for. The identification was in the male name but he had accepted the Mr and Mrs from the man alone. My guess would be that the name Tully is way off the mark. Really nothing to go on except the car registration, if he managed to record it correctly!'

2

'And so, my dear Tony, you are up to date with all that happened to me last evening. I hope I have not omitted anything of importance or over elaborated on detail. You will not offend if you surmise that I must have been at the bottle or dreamt it all. I find it hard to believe myself'.

Sitting opposite me, was Anthony Fairchild, twenty nine-ish, a trifle under six feet, athletically slim and with mid brown hair. Whilst the face would not, perhaps, have inspired the launch of even a canal barge it was nevertheless, reasonably handsome. And there, any resemblance between us is proved to be non-existent.

Just in case we haven't been introduced: I'm Diamond, Roger Diamond, and stifle the cracks about 'jewel', 'brilliant' and especially 'flasher'. I've heard them all before. 'Diamond is a girl's best friend' bears no resemblance to the general trend of my social life, so forget it. About an inch taller than Tony and, whilst fat or even plump would bring a frown, I would agree to 'a little heavier than he'. Hair dark, but I have recently commenced combing it to the side rather than back from the forehead, if you know what I mean. Nothing more than a couple of months difference in our ages and we are friends, firm friends, from way back.

The whole of the previous, and for me sleepless, night had allowed an acceptance of the shock engendered by the events experienced in Fergie's room. But for Tony there had only been the minutes taken by me to relate such of the episode that I had been sufficiently conscious to recall. Looking across at him I could see the changed expression, indicating a dawning realisation of potential danger, particularly for Fergie.

'I tried to contact Fergie last evening,' I informed him. 'He had not been to his flat at all. This morning I decided to chance a message to Personnel to the effect that Fergie wished to report himself sick. As soon as I got through the girl was eager to be the first to tell me that Mr Ferguson had suffered a family bereavement and would be taking two weeks back leave. In reply to my question she said that he had made the call himself and within the previous ten minutes. So that gives us a short while to sort out Fergie and his troubles before an official report has to be entertained, let alone acted upon. What do you think?'

'Thank God for a little time,' Tony replied. 'But is it Fergie's trouble we hope to unravel or is Fergie part of it all?. It cannot be anyone but he who drugged your coffee. I stress that because we have to decide, as soon as it is practicable, whether we hold Fergie to be a victim, or a conspirator in this melodramatic clique with their stupid coded messages. Confessions and Cardinals indeed! If it were not for the gun I would laugh my head off. Fergie certainly has knowledge of what it is all about, hence his successful effort to get you, unwittingly, to keep his appointment with the eventual callers. Now, we both know our man and in knowing him can rest assured that the only way he could be connected with anything other than honest, open and above board, would be as a result of a particularly nasty blackmail. One cannot easily ascribe an emotional phrase to someone with our friend's strength of character but 'a cry for help' is a description that comes to mind. We are both officers of the Court and have much to lose as a result of an attempted cover up. Leaving the gun aside, is there anything in what happened to you last evening that we must report now to our superiors? Later could, of course, be quite a different matter.'

12

'It is of course possible for Fergie to have planned and managed the whole timetable of events,' I commented. 'Those two went there by appointment, exactly as they informed the man at the check point. My entry and the coffee were timed sufficiently early for me to give every appearance of being sloshed by the time they entered. I think something like valium could have produced that effect, particularly the colourful hallucination.'

'Yes, indeed,' from a nodding Tony. 'And motives,' he continued.

'Fergie wanted to bring to your attention first hand, something that he is up against or threatened by, rather than ask directly for your help, which he knew would be forthcoming but felt was not merited. And the motive of the two, as you tag them, and their associates could be blackmail, to coerce Fergie to do something he is unwilling to do. Just how sinister is the project towards which those acts are intended to contribute I cannot guess.'

I had asked Tony to meet me for three very good reasons: he is a sound and dependable friend; he is also a true friend to Fergie and most importantly he is a Queen's Bench Officer, thoroughly skilled in sifting and exploring evidence in criminal cases. I hold a similar position in the Chancery Division but had already sensed we may well be looking at matters of a criminal nature. As an extra bonus his father, Sir Brian Fairchild, is the police chief for Surrey, operating from headquarters at Guildford.

During a pause, and as I reflected on all of the happenings, I recalled a detail I had first set aside. Turning to Tony, I said:

'Among the many things with which I mentally grappled during the long night I came to see something as a message from Fergie to me, to us. But in much the same way as you were unimpressed by the seemingly childish coded messages, I judged my discovery to be a bit of a nonsense from our friend. I am now convinced that it was a serious message from a very serious person and feel sure you will find it worthy of investigation. Remember I mentioned my attempt at upside down reading of papers on Fergie's desk? One document was so placed, to guarantee that it would catch my attention. It was at the rear of the desk and I could read it with ease, the right way up.

Thinking it to be for our eyes only I placed it in my pocket, but unfortunately this is not the suit.

It was a receipted invoice for a motor car service, a printed form and headed: Mastersons of Balham. The work was itemised but no reference made to the vehicle registration number, although further down the invoice there was a bold entry made in biro, with typically Fergie flourish, B 495 URG. Now, he has never had a vehicle of that registration number, so do you agree that the hurried, covert message to us is intended to read: "Before the ninth of May — URGENT." And as he went to the length of finding an old invoice, could it have something to do with Mastersons or their premises?'

'It has, of course it has,' Tony said excitedly, 'but that is just a large show room on the Balham High Road.'

'No, I accompanied Fergie there on one occasion, the workshops are at the rear, on the little road that runs parallel. Quite ramshackle compared with the gleaming appearance of the sales showrooms, but equally extensive.'

We had used up almost all of our lunch period and were arranging to carry on at five o'clock, or earlier if our duties would allow, when my telephone rang. I took the call. It was the Inspector in charge of the police office within the building. Putting down the telephone I said:

'Tony, the car — the Montego, it's registered to Gino Morrelli, head waiter at the Italian restaurant just along the Strand.'

Before parting we resolved to continue our deliberation

later that afternoon.

We were back together at a few minutes after five o'clock. My room is on the second floor of the Royal Courts of Justice in the Strand. You probably know it, not my room of course, the building. Tony had telephoned his wife, Carol and, at his suggestion, she was expecting us for a very early evening meal. He proposed, and I agreed, we tell her some of the importance of what had happened. Not so much that it would worry her unduly but sufficient to let her know that to answer Fergie's unconventional plea could lead to enquiries at very odd places, and certainly at unusual hours.

As we prepared to leave for his home, and in what appeared to be an afterthought, Tony said:

'Is there anything in what has happened that necessitates a report to the powers that be, even now, by telephone?'

'No, I don't think so, although I have a creeping suspicion that it may become so. But for the present all we have is, Fergie receiving a private visit at his place of work out of office hours. Perfectly permissable. And the next day takes a period of back leave, for personal reasons.'

'Still, as you mentioned, there is the matter of the gun.' Tony seemed to be thinking out loud. 'The security bod dropped a clanger there. He, of course, deserves to have his knuckles rapped but weighed against the harm that might be done, quite unnecessarily, to Fergie's future, I am not sure.'

'Exactly.' I looked appreciatively towards Tony. 'And if it will help to salve the moral tenderness of each of us, I was very woozy at the time and women have been known to carry lighters, in their handbags, which look remarkably like hand guns.'

Carol prepared my favourite 'off the peg' fast-food — an English breakfast. Even nicer, I think, when eaten in the early evening. It seems that whenever I visit their

15

delightful little place in Kennington I ruefully think of how a broken engagement three years back separated me from their kind of bliss. It is then that I hurriedly console myself with thoughts of couples who's relationships could never convince me that marriage is the ultimate happiness.

We acquainted Carol with our version of events. With typical female reaction she said:

'Is there more?'

We also agreed that the Italian head waiter and Mastersons posed queries we should tackle right away.

The meal finished, I said to Tony:

'Shall we take one enquiry each to save time? One to the restaurant, the other to Mastersons?'

'Fine,' he answered. But surely the show room will be closed?'

'That's so. But there is accommodation above and one could glean information just nosing around and chatting with the locals, especially if there is a bar nearby.'

'Yes, of course, the cleverly disguised message suggests a softly, softly approach and certainly not direct confrontation — well, not to begin with, if at all.'

'Predictable Fergie, using an unobtrusive article to guard a message intended only for us. Did I tell you that the date of the invoice was almost twelve months ago? I do sometimes wish that I had such a tidy, methodical mind. Now, Tony, which job do you prefer to tackle?'

Carol chipped in with:

'Plain clothes police go around in pairs. If you go together you will probably get the answers you seek without continually having to explain who you are. And Roger, I want Tony to be the Chief Inspector, the pay is so much better!'

We chuckled and Tony said:

'Right then Sergeant, let's go.'

As we made to leave I caught a glance from Carol

towards Tony which I thought mildly expressed a 'take care', and some relief that we would be working together. Possibly our revelation to her of the previous day's affair and particularly the thought of the gun was now uppermost in her mind.

3

Gino Morrelli was an amiable man and most accommodating. As the night was still young and business correspondingly thin he was more than willing to answer questions about his car. Tony, seeking to set him at ease from the start, said:

'Of course, when people make a mental note of the index number of a car connected with an incident, there is massive room for error.'

Gino said: 'F 468 GNK is the number of my car and my car is a Montego, but metallic grey'. I caught the averted glance from Tony as Morelli continued. 'It was not in use at the time you say. Every evening I drive it to the meter bays, just beyond the reserved area at Australia House. The day folks are just off home then and I get in quite easily, very often it will be at the same meter. I always pay for one hour which takes me on to the free parking, and there it stays until the early hours, usually two o'clock, when I return home. The staff will tell you I am always here at around five-forty, having walked from the car.'

In answer to Tony's final question he said: 'I have never given anyone permission to take my car, from there or anywhere else. I have an owner driver only policy. My wife doesn't drive.'

We thanked him profusely and, as there were some empty tables, asked if we might stay just long enough to have coffee.

Once settled I said: 'Is he lying? Did he visit Fergie's room? If he did he is a damned good actor, because, whilst I couldn't see the intruder, he saw a hell of a lot of me

18

and this guy didn't even twitch when we came face to face. Did he park very much later last evening? Staff will usually support a boss when it comes to statements and what about the rapid reference to metallic grey?'

'Personally I would find it difficult to associate Gino with anything more sinister than watering my beer,' Tony ventured. 'Earlier you put forward a theory that in my opinion was not far from correct. Now, will you try this for probabilities: He leaves his car in the same place day in, day out. Someone gets to realise this, it could be staff, anyone working nearby, or a person prepared to stand there and take stock of opportunities. That someone, or persons informed by that someone, are going to visit Fergie to pile on the pressure. They drive to the parking space, pull Gino's car out leaving their own to hold the place, returning later when the change over is reversed. They know Gino's habits and so they have all the time in the world. My, one could use the idea to provide a confusing get-away car when breaking into the Bank of England.'

'Good, very good. I go along with that, but what about car keys?'

'Not too difficult if you have the essential.'

'What is the essential?'

'Money, and enough of it,' he replied. 'A shady main dealer or, much more likely, an employee whose wages are not sufficiently high to present him or her with a loyalty embarrassment. A visit to the parking site with the sets of manufacturers masters. Ten minutes and you have it or them. A key cutting job and the finished product is exchanged for a little stack of notes.'

I did say how good it was to have his Queen's Bench knowledge of criminal habit didn't I!

So the field was wide open, but we were both fairly sure that Gino would not be coming into the final reckoning.

4

As I do not care a lot for conversation when I am driving, I gave the same consideration to Tony and the journey to Balham was made in almost complete silence.

On our arrival, Mastersons was much as we had expected. The showrooms were closed and there was no reply to ringing and knocking at the doors to the accommodation above. In Sillet Street, at the rear, we found the workshop area to be large, corresponding to the four terraced shop area of the showroom on the main road.

There were three sets of double doors, secured together with clasps and each fastened by a massive padlock. It was all single storey and the roof was corrugated, but in the poorly lit area it was difficult to be certain whether of iron or asbestos. At one end, however, there was a section which was more soundly constructed, with close fitting key-locked doors and a facia board above, which suggested a more conventional flat roof.

On the opposite side of the street there was a small warehouse and with Tony supporting me I was able to stand on a window sill and get a somewhat restricted view of Masterson's workshops. I could see at one end a sound flat roof with a built up sky-light which was slightly in the raised position.

'A good time to make a search?' I questioned and I could tell that Tony was keen, even before he answered. We decided that I would stay on the road as a lookout. You will recall that Tony is the athletic one.

'There may well be an open yard between here and the showroom but only go down if you are sure of a way back,'

I said although aware that he would know just what he was, or was not, prepared to take on.

He put the side of one shoe on to the staple and padlock combined. I managed to assist him up until his hands clung to the edge of the roof. I held him there, with upward pressure under his buttocks, whilst he slowly raised first one foot and then the other, until he was standing on my shoulders. I shall do my best to forget the number of times that his shoe made rough contact with my ears.

It was, of course, corrugated iron roofing and adopting a half crouched stance and ape-like movement he made his way to the truly flat roof. He had, I knew, his fountain-pen type pocket torch with him but would not be likely to use it for fear of drawing attention to our actions.

A little earlier than I had expected he was back at the roof edge and from the animated gesticulation I surmised that he had been discovered. I extended my arms upward and as he crouched well forward stretching one hand downward I was able to clasp it with both of mine and he made an agile leap to the ground. His face was ashen, as if in shock, but his movements and utterance of the words 'Come, come,' indicated great excitement. I moved with him in the direction he prodded me, all the while listening and looking for whoever, or whatever, could be following.

At the corner of Sillet Street with Crown Road which leads back to the High Road he seemed content to slow down and then to stop.

He blurted out: 'Roger, what the hell is Fergie caught up in? And into what bloody mess have we just taken two steps towards becoming involved?'

It was as though he had been previously afraid of being overheard and that now the outpouring of words must flow or he would burst.

'The security van, Roger, the one that was hijacked on the bank run, two weeks ago, ambushed and stolen. It is in there and it is being resprayed.'

'Steady, just a minute, Tony. From the rapid retreat I imagined that you had been seen. Should we not be heading away fast?'

'Yes, it might be wise to move on a little. I did not see or hear anyone, but did have the feeling that I was being watched and I thought the watcher must have been more afraid than I and so remained silent.'

We walked hastily on to the High Road. There is a pub on the other side but at my suggestion we made for the car as the best possible place to resume talking without being overheard. Before getting in we tidied ourselves, fingers brushing at the dirt on our clothes. For me it was only the shoulders and top of my jacket but Tony was filthy from his coat to his shoes. However we soon looked reasonably presentable.

In the car Tony expanded on what he had seen from the roof. Once again speaking excitedly as he recalled the drama of those few minutes.

'There was a small crack to one corner of a pane of glass forming a triangle. Using my penknife I was able to prize out that piece. Placing the end of the torch through the hole and moving it around, it cast sufficient light to give me a fairly comprehensive view of the paint shop below and the vehicle in it. There was no mistaking that it is the security van, although an undoubtedly experienced sheet-metal worker has removed the top air-vent. Also, the small windows to the sides and the rear were skillfully filled in with metal. When the respray is complete Mr and Mrs Average will not recognise it standing at the kerbside three feet from them!'

'I think it would be fair to say the reference to the ninth of May in Fergie's message is the date by which the job has to be finished and the van ready for who knows where. What do you think? Can it be ready by then?' I asked.

'Oh yes, sure' Tony replied 'It was clear an orderly work schedule was in progress. There were two long wide boards to one side and, although I could not clearly see, I feel sure that there was a traders name on them and they will, I guess, be bolted one to each side. Just another piece of camouflage.'

'And would you say that, even if it isn't in the van at the moment, the loot will be transported in it?'

'Why not? Now that they have got as far as they have it must be safer, from their point of view, than breaking up the load, thus increasing the number of people in the know.'

He had just finished his sentence when the door beside me jerked open and a large man peered in and said 'Do you know Sillet Street, off Crown Road,' in a gruff voice that matched the unpleasant look on his face.

I surprised myself with quickness of thought and replied 'Sorry, we are strangers here.'

'Hanging around like that I thought you must be locals,' and with that he left.

'That was to see if we had been roof climbing, wouldn't you say? And do you think it is time we made our visit to the pub before heading for home?'

'Yes, yes,' added Tony. 'But do you think that he suspects us? And if so should we not be halfway home by now, planning a new line of enquiry for tomorrow?'

'Nothing to lose by staying,' I replied. 'Looking on the blackside, he already has your index number and can trace us from that. On the bright side he is, I think, a long way from being sure about us. So let's go, eh?'

A decision as to saloon or public bar proved immaterial as a conversion had merged them into one. Modernly but not over-comfortably furnished and with wipe clean tables and chairs, it was quite pleasant.

We stood at the bar in the hope of partaking in light local

conversation. After opening pleasantries I asked if Mastersons were still doing car repairs.

'I used to be with them,' said one man. 'What repairs have you in mind?'

'Well, actually, I need a really good respray. There are not many places left where one can get a first class job!'

Tony's toe pressed the side of my foot. I had myself noticed the sudden glance from the man behind the bar at the mention of a respray and that he had left the bar immediately afterwards. I carried on conversing with my helpful friend. He was not sure about respray prices but felt sure they were still doing a bit. After I had bought him a pint he continued to tell what it was like to work there. But that was before Mastersons had paid him off. 'On account of age, they said, but I still had good work in me. They wanted to bring in their new men.'

He was still talking when I noticed two large men coming into the bar. One was the caller at the car earlier. A tug at my sleeve and I was sure that Tony was equally aware of our visitors.

The one we had met pushed his way between my new found friend and myself, the other moved in close to Tony.

Without stopping to order drinks the one beside me said: 'You two seem to be poking your noses into things around here.'

I tried to outstare him and said: 'Do you mind! I am making some enquiries about work on my car.'

'Mr Masterson does business direct. Face to face in his office and not through sneaky little chats in a pub. Now drink your beer and get off or I will call the coppers.'

Realising that attack is the best defence I said: 'Do just that, brother, and when our colleagues arrive they will, no doubt, want to know why you are showing so much interest in us.'

It did the trick.

They both moved well down the bar, had a small beer with the barman and, a short while later, left.

As we made our way to the car, and with Tony nodding agreement, I said: 'It is getting a bit over our heads. I think the next move must be a chat with your Dad. He is the very man to help outline any future activity.'

Tony dropped me off at the little boarding house at the rear of Lincoln's Inn Fields in which I have lived since coming to London.

With agreement to be in touch on the morrow he headed off to Kennington, and Carol.

The next morning Tony telephoned early, so early that I had not yet gone down to breakfast, to tell me that his father had invited the two of us and Carol to spend the weekend at his home at Merrow. Tony said that he had briefly informed his father of the events of the two previous evenings. Sir Brian had replied that the weekend would allow time for us to expand upon our little problem. He also said that he would be inviting the Commissioner of the Metropolitan force to lunch on the Saturday or Sunday, whichever was more convenient.

I told Tony how pleased and relieved I was that official authorities would be taking over but added concern that Fergie should have some protection in case the two who had called upon me in his room, turned really nasty as a result of official action. We both expressed certainty that Fergie himself would not have had any part in anything unlawful.

Turning to travel arrangements I asked what time we were expected the next day.

'Around eleven.'

'O.K. I will pick you up at ten. It will be my turn to provide the wheels and if anyone is keeping tabs, a different car and index leaving your place is a good move.'

'Thanks. Put your clubs in, we may manage to get in

a round at the old man's club. All work and no play, no good for what ails you.'

'Fine. I'll see you then if not before, at the factory today.'

5

During the previous somewhat sleepless night, I had gone over events and the possible predicament they suggested Fergie might be in. I recalled that some four or five months earlier Norman Cartwright, of accounts, had left very suddenly. Fergie's remark at the time was: 'He was hounded out, make no mistake, he was hounded out.' I now found the words capable of a different connotation than I had thought at the time.

I hurried breakfast and went to the courts building immediately. As I was earlier than usual the place was almost deserted, although offices and rooms were open to allow cleaners freedom of movement.

I walked through the Tower Block, one of the few buildings consisting entirely of offices, and came to the little personnel office. I suppose I refer to it as the little office not so much on account of it being a small room, but because the main personnel department is housed within the Lord Chancellor's department. The one I had entered is concerned only with records of those actively engaged at the Royal Courts of Justice.

I went directly to the filing cabinet clearly marked 'C'. The information entered on individual cards was meagre, name, address, next of kin, blood group etc and intended only for emergencies. I was looking for an address and, if possible, a telephone number, so the cards would be perfectly adequate.

My fingers were threading and my eyes scanning through them when a shrill, no, not so much shrill, but commanding voice spat words at me as if firing bullets

27

from an automatic pistol.

'What the hell are you doing at those cabinets?'

I turned and saw what surely must be the most beautiful female to have come into my life. Not pretty and warm and nice, like Tony's Carol and so many other girls, but with cold, chisled features, statuesque posture, assured almost arrogant tilt of the head and eyes that conveyed perhaps not contempt but certainly a measure of disdain. But with all of that, very very beautiful.

'Exactly as it should appear,' I coldly snapped back. 'I am looking for a card upon which I hope to find the forwarding address of someone who has left the department.'

The pistol recommenced firing: 'Those are confidential documents. Confidential to and between the individual and the department.'

'Balls,' I shouted back. I think that the desire to use an inelegant word sprang from astonishment at the verbal attack and concern at the poor start I had made to what might have been a very rewarding acquaintance.

'If you want files and confidentiality you go to Neville House,' I continued, 'but if it is just an address you seek, you can easily find it here. And if the information is so confidential why were the blasted cabinets not locked?'

'This is not my section, although I have a higher overall responsibility. Where those of your rank and standing are concerned we can surely expect ethics and morals to influence actions. There must be and there are rules of conduct if only to curtail male chauvinists from using the records to maintain contact with their floozies.'

'I was in fact seeking a forwarding address for Norman Cartwright who, until recently, was on the staff.'

The name brought a direct look from her towards me. She probably knew him. Her attitude appeared to moderate a little. However, she continued her would-be reprimand saying: 'I shall have to report this you know. It calls for a clear cut directive.'

I cannot be sure if my decision to take her partially into my confidence was prompted by a wish to avoid inter-departmental censure notes or a full blown desire to continue in her company.

I told her, in only very limited detail, of two incidents from the happenings, as I had to begun to call them, in order to link them to my need for information about Cartwright. She was an attentive listener and used the odd word or phrase to express interest, which I found most encouraging. She still maintained, however, that she must report the matter.

Bearing in mind that the police were about to come in on it, I said 'You must do what you must do but as I am to be reported for my crime I will partake of the fruits by looking up Cartwright on the card.' Unfortunately the address shown was the one he had used whilst working with us.

Just before two o'clock the chief registrar contacted me with a message: I was to be at the House of Lords at four-thirty that afternoon to be interviewed by the Lord Chancellor.

I thought it could not possibly be as a result of the little skirmish with — and I realised that I did not know her name. Anyway, it was not of the stuff with which Lord Chancellor's soil their hands.

I left for the Lords at four o'clock and at two minutes to the half hour the personal secretary was showing me into the Lord Chancellor's room. And there I had my second shock of the day for sitting in front of the desk with an empty chair beside her was Miss You Know Who — or was it Mrs? It was all smiles and hello.

'Madam,' I thought, 'there is either a chink in your character or a big hole in mine. Vinegar in the morning and syrup eight hours later do not mix, but you are you and I am glad to be here to receive your smiles.'

Lord Garland answered my poser of a moment before when he said: 'Good to see you Diamond. You have met Miss Mandrake, Helen Mandrake, before, and only very recently I understand.'

Not a man I could take to. Far too much self adoration. Yet here he was, all sweetness and light.

'As you were no doubt busy with court duties, I asked Miss Mandrake to acquaint me with the startling, no alarming, events of the past few days. Do you think it an attempt to involve the department generally or the courts in particular?'

As I had not mentioned the security van, Fergie's clue to Mastersons or the advent of police intervention to Helen, I was able clearly to answer: 'Neither, I view the whole matter as a personal one between Mr Ferguson and the callers.' The quick witted Helen was in like a flash with 'How do you draw a connection between that and Mr Cartwright?'

'Not very clearly, I replied slowly, adding: 'But I assumed, that by innuendo, they wished to infer that Mr Ferguson was responsible for the departure of Mr Cartwright.'

I suppressed a sigh of relief when they both appeared to accept such a wildly off-target explanation.

There then appeared to be a complete change of approach as Lord Garland said: 'You, Diamond, have been brought into this matter by circumstances not very much removed from chance. Let me say straight away, I am of the opinion that you have handled the situation and yourself very well indeed. Excellent, excellent. But, as to the immediate future, I am anxious no inference is made that all is not well within the department. To bring in new faces, either the police or enquiry agents will only alarm the staff.

I am, therefore asking you now, if you are prepared to carry out discreet enquiries to establish whether there is any behaviour that might have an adverse effect on the honest, open and scrupulously fair conduct of department business. If your answer is yes, then spare no effort in finding out and revealing the identity of the perpetrators.

I have, however, one condition. Miss Mandrake must work closely with you throughout. Many advantages suggest themselves. You must accept from me that she is of exemplary character and has a very active, fertile mind and high intellect.

You should adopt and simulate a workplace, romantic, friendship which will allow you to be seen together talking quietly or animatedly, without drawing attention to yourselves. If you both agree to my proposal I will arrange that you have carte blanche regarding movement and travel as well as cover, according to your needs, at any given time.

Now Helen, er, Miss Mandrake, I think that you should first have the right to say whether or not you are prepared to work with this young fellow.'

'I think it an interesting challenge to find out what, if anything, is amiss. I am sure that it will be demanding and time consuming so that whether or not we are socially at one is immaterial. Our individual judgements will not be impaired. In physical appearance we are acceptable as characters in the assignment you set. So I see every prospect of success. Yes, I accept.'

Lord Garland glanced in my direction. I said: 'The lady has said it all. I too accept.'

'Two more points,' said his Lordship. 'First I do not expect or want you to refer matters to me. You will, between you, come to conclusions as to the best way to proceed and we will know, or rather you will know, when your efforts have produced the answers we seek. Second, and lastly, I wish you success with your venture. I hope that you enjoy working together. To start it off aright why not take Miss Mandrake out to dinner tonight? If you will make it Romanoffs, where I am at least known, I will telephone and arrange to pick up the bill.'

I looked across at Helen. Her beautiful face smilingly expressed acquiescence.

The evening was a fabulous success. Helen had asked me to collect her from the court building. Breathtaking was the only adequate way to describe the sight as she came to meet me. The ivory satin dress, of classical lines, featured the natural elegance of Helen herself. The pride I felt at that moment was later enhanced as I observed just how many male heads were turned by her presence. Helen acted as though unaware of the glances and devoted every moment, at the table and while dancing, to sharing the happiness we found in the company of each other.

The restaurant, the unobtrusive but friendly attention of the staff, and of course, the food provided an ambience which for me brought new meaning to the delight of eating out. That was how I felt, the magic of Helen stimulated joy and excitement I had not previously experienced and I knew, beyond any doubt, that I was, and would always be, in love with her.

However, there was a minor set-back for me when a Cinderella occurrence signalled the end of our fantastic first date. I had beckoned the head waiter in order to request that a taxi be arranged. When he came to us it was Helen who said:

'May we have two cabs?'

There was, nevertheless, consolation when I stood at the door of her taxi thanking her for such a wonderful evening.

'I could ask for nothing more than to always be your escort.'

She placed her hand upon mine and said:

'I know. And you will, Roger, you will.'

As she was driven away I realised that I was looking forward to my whole future with anticipation.

6

The drive through south London and into Surrey was particularly pleasant. The second of May had brought with it a perfect day, staking a claim to rival those of the summer still to come. Carol and Tony sat in the back of the car chatting on a variety of topics, seeking any other than the one we had determined to avoid until we handed our self-imposed commitment over to the police for solution. And that we were about to do.

All of which left me with uninterrupted time. Time I would have sought anyway. Time to think of Helen and recall the joyous moments of the previous evening.

Then, the conversation at the table had been so very stimulating. Helen, whose in-depth knowledge of many subjects soon became apparent, took pains to ensure that there was, at all times, an exchange of views. I was terrifically impressed by her complete grasp of current affairs, both domestic and global, expressing as she did her alternative themes for seeking and obtaining new balances of power in the wake of the dissolution of the Soviet Republic. It was her view that a lessening of widely held firm policy coming from the United States provided an opportunity and indeed a duty upon Europe, and Britain in particular, to engender a new balance of power; that for the Russians to endure a sense of inferiority could make for a dangerous situation.

Had the leaders of political parties been as flies upon the wall to hear and appreciate the command of the subject displayed by Helen they would, like me, have realised there was a ready made female leader of the future, at least equal to the one who had held sway for so long.

The chat while dancing, however, was light and gay and I got a surprising come-uppance when I chose to mention the excellence of Helen's dress.

I facetiously added: 'You made it yourself, of course?.

To which she replied 'No. Madame Corbin is a wonderful dressmaker. She is also a good friend and allows me to do my own designs.'

Not just a beautiful face, this young lady whom I intended to woo and win! I was full of admiration for her many talents and recognising the glow of happiness within me I was content to fall victim to her undoubted fascination.

We were passing an exit spur when the road signs indicated Send and Woking and memories holding very mixed emotions came flooding back to me. This stretch of country was fairly new to Carol and Tony. They had lived in Leicestershire until Sir Brian Fairchild, Tony's father, had been appointed Chief Constable of the Surrey force.

For me it was another sentimental trip to scenes of firstly, schoolboy games of Cowboys and Indians or war battles, either or both, fought out in the disused sandpit, closely followed, it seemed, by teenage rambling, family picnics and in due time a hand-in-hand stroll with that very first girl-friend, both of us still in the sixth form. I had been born in Send and lived there happily with my parents until a tragic road accident had taken them both from me in one very cruel moment, six years earlier.

From that time Tony and I had become firm friends. His father, Brian, as he insists I call him, and Betty his mother have fussed over me as they would have another son.

Before long we were driving through Merrow and the two in the back began showing excited interest as they realised how close we were to Mum and Dad, and as I turned the car into the short driveway they were coming from the house to greet us. Once inside and for a while thereafter there was a typical exchange of family news and views. From their animated conversation it was difficult to appreciate that Carol and Betty had spoken together on the telephone three times during the past seven days, with each call of more than thirty minutes duration! But it was not long before I noticed Betty gently edging the younger woman away, leaving we three males together. She knew from experience that invitations for lunch at her home could have quite a different purpose than merely a pleasant social gathering.

The reason for the early departure of the ladies became apparent when Brian informed us that the Commissioner would be arriving shortly and would have with him Roy Newbold, the new Home Secretary.

'They both have other week-end engagements and in order to pack everything into the time available I will do my best to explain how certain facts of what Tony told me over the telephone, coincide with feedback from our own men. Taken together they form a pattern giving cause for concern.'

When imparting information of a classified or confidential nature, Brian has a habit of taking his listeners out into the open while giving his news to them. He says it is a hangover from his days in H.M. Forces when there was every possibility that a room, office or even a whole barracks had been bugged. So while continuing to talk he led us out into the garden, walking us around the lawns and beds. An enthusiastic gardener, by doing so he had the additional bonus of seeing admiring glances and hearing appreciative murmurings as we went.

'Our reports,' he went on, 'Suggest a nationwide association. Quite secretive in nature. Until now there has been no information disclosing the possession or use of arms. A political pressure group is one theory and a scheme to instil pride of citizenship is another. I don't find either credible. The type of person engaged in those pastimes is ultra-enthusiastic and anti-secretive. He will give you his name and address without being asked. Of course, where the project is financed only by the weekly or monthly contributions of members, there can be no serious potential either for good or evil. If however, there are large injections of cash from one, or only a few wealthy persons, we are duty bound to query the motive of the doner or doners.

I know our visitors intend to ask you both if you will continue to exploit the advantage of being at the heart of whatever is happening without arousing the suspicion new faces would engender. As a policeman I wholeheartedly go along with the request but as your father I want to counsel caution. You are also in the firing line and over enthusiastic inquisitiveness could make that a very dangerous place to be.'

After seemingly no time at all we were moving into the hall to meet the special guests. Sir John Embury, the Commissioner, I had met on a couple of previous occasions. Looking now at his face I could see a few careworn lines I had not noticed before and wondered how much longer he would have to carry out his onerous task in London before he was entitled to a well deserved retirement. When he got to me and was shaking my hand, he said:

'Now Roger, when are you going to make one young lady deliriously happy at the expense of so many?' With a broad grin on my face, I replied:

'It is funny you should say that, Sir.'

'Ho! ho! So it has happened. You must come to the Yard and tell me all about her.'

Sir John is six feet, three inches tall and seemingly dwarfed the Home Secretary, who I would guess to be a very presentable five feet nine. Roy Newbold, an amiable

Yorkshireman had a long sojourn in the Ministry for the Environment before being, somewhat surprisingly, pitchforked into his high office some six months previously. When I had an opportunity to congratulate him, in thanking me he said:

'It's a bit like being placed in a goldfish bowl, with more than a few eyes looking in to see if I trip and fall.'

A very agreeable light lunch and right on cue Betty invited Carol to join her in a walk to the village. And so we were now five men together for the purpose of exchanging information and ideas.

I ran through the circumstances of my disturbing evening in Fergie's room and of our clearing Gino of blame concerning the undoubted use of his car at that time. Tony took over to the extraordinary events at Mastersons and of the menacing moments at the car and in the pub.

I then recited the reasons for our certainty that the words of the aside 'How is your dear friend John, by the way?' was a prepared, surreptitious threat made with the intention of putting the greatest pressure on Fergie. I gave my opinion that it referred to Father John Giles of the Roman Catholic Church at Marylebone. I explained how Fergie had confided to me the very great affection he and the Father had for one another. Whilst not proud of his feelings, neither was he ashamed, and as a consequence I was sure he was not at risk of blackmail. But if harm, shame or threat of defrocking were convincingly uttered in respect of the Father, Fergie might well be brought to breaking point. I told them that my decision to breach his confidence was to demonstrate the lengths and depths the bastards, whoever they were, would go to break the will of an honourable man.

I went on to tell them of Norman Cartwright and how Tony had, at last, been able to find an address in Chester le Street. Of my new found belief in the real reason for

Cartwright's sudden departure, confirmed, as it was, by Fergie's words to me: 'He was hounded out, make no mistake, he was hounded out.' I asserted that if Tony and I could get to him early enough, our past association might offer sufficient assurance for him to reveal something of what was going on. Brian said:

'I could lay on a helicopter to get you there tomorrow.'

He turned to the Home Secretary, who nodded emphatically.

'There you are then,' Brian continued, 'tomorrow it is. I will make the arrangements when we have finished here. You can take off right after dawn if you wish. Betty and I will look forward to Carol staying on with us if she is willing and perhaps she could drive your car back, Roger. I could then have you two dropped off at the South Bank helicopter base, on your return.'

'And now Minister, Sir John,' he said, addressing them together, 'I know from our telephone conversations earlier that you have proposals as to how these two young men can best help to further our enquiries.'

I hastened to intervene:

'Before you do so, Gentlemen, and as it may well have a bearing on your decision, I should tell you of an arrangement I agreed with Lord Garland. May I?'

Receiving a nod from each of them I went on to recount my unfortunate first meeting with Helen and the subsequent interview with the Lord Chancellor.

'Speaking for myself I would say that far from being in conflict, the arrangement would appear to complement the proposals I had agreed with Sir John,' said Mr Newbold, 'I will, however, leave it to him to elucidate as he will have overall control of the operation, if that is not too gradely a description, as we Yorkshire folk might say, of what will be co-operation between police and public to fight crime.'

Sir John, unhampered by the constraints of political

posturing, was very much to the point:

'I hope that you will continue as you have been. I could not and do not ask for more; if and when the time comes for risks to be taken we will be the ones to come in to take them. I could not be more pleased than to have you both already set in the target area, as we in the force might say.' This with a wry grin in the direction of the Home Secretary. 'And having, as Brian the gardener would say, the anonymity of primroses in a bog garden. Lord Garland's approach to you is a godsend but I must insist, do not pass information you may gather either to him or to the girl before you have reported it to the officer allocated for the purpose, for vetting. Do not misunderstand me. I know nothing against either of them, nothing at all, but from what you tell me of the girl she has no track record of responsibility, real accountability I mean. And Jack Garland, full of charm, not only sees reds under beds, he is convinced there are reds under every bed but his own; sufficiently paranoid at times to quote confidential information in support of a contention that anyone but he is subversive.

Now to the practicalities of my request that you liaise with me through the officers I will assign to each of you. Please use them to keep abreast of the situation as we understand it to be and to seek help that you may need. Use them every bit for your own purposes as well as for passing information on. I cannot tell you who they will be for the simple reason that I do not know, but they will contact you on Monday. No attempt will be made to contact you at your homes, one new caller there may draw a lot of attention to his or herself, whereas asking for you at your courts building is a very forgettable item in a busy attendants day. Do not be surprised by the manner of the visit: a man in overalls calling to collect your car for repair or service will far less attract recall than one in a pin-striped

40

suit selling insurance.

We are taking the unusual step of asking for your co-operation because the ingenious scheme so cleverly executed by Mr Ferguson led you to discover the menacing threats used by members of this organisation without drawing attention to yourselves. The secret manner in which it has been started and continues recruitment calls into question the bona-fides of the association itself and more importantly those of its founders. There is every reason to suppose there are activists among staff members of the courts service; we have the plus that you are both on site and Roger, the result of your little contretemps with the girl is a first class bonus. With Lord Garland's blessing you are a free range chick!

A final word of caution. The proceeds of crime are a frequent source of funding illegal organisations. Crime is committed by criminals. When cornered criminals become very nasty. I cannot improve on the advice we give to our young bobby on the beat: do not go in until you have sent a message requesting back up. Our best wishes go with you both of course, and our sincere thanks.'

Only the exchange of fond farewells remained before they left and Brian, Tony and I sped away to Brian's golf club.

7

At about eight o'clock the following morning Brian drove us all to where the helicopter was housed. It was already out on the pad and within minutes Tony and I were waving goodbye before being whisked northward.

'I thought that Carol was pretty marvellous when she learned that we were to continue as Holmes and Watson; she must, like us, have thought that this week-end was the finish of it all,' I said and Tony immediately replied, with a chuckle:

'She is a great lass, all she asked is that I let her have an up to date photograph of myself to ensure that she does not unknowingly pass me in the street!'

Down to earth literally and in a taxi heading for the Cartwright home we began to speculate as to how much information Norman could and would impart to us. We reminded ourselves of his promotion, with its conditional transfer to London creating the initial problem for him, which eventually got so out of hand. His wife, Rene, was not enamoured with the thought of London and its environs and had emphatically insisted that any move should be to a home of equal amenity.

The taxi pulled to the kerb; we stood and admired the detached house surrounded by average sized well designed and neatly kept gardens. Without having seen the interior I was convinced that to replace it in the London area, would cost three times its selling price. Tony said: 'Who could blame her? Any woman would have set tough terms for leaving.'

We were greeted warmly but also I thought a little

apprehensively. Rene brought coffee and biscuits from the kitchen.

'You must have lunch here with us, I have a roast in the oven.' A little later she excused herself with: 'I will leave you men to talk.'

Cartwright said: 'Everything I can tell you, she knows already. She wishes to spare me the embarrassment of repeating it while she is present.' 'A wife to be proud of.' Tony said with understanding.

Tony, ever the one to put a person at ease was at once engaged in gentle conversation with Norman.

'Even as we talked over the phone, I knew you were aware of the reason for our call,' he was saying. 'After the trauma of the threat to Mr Ferguson and his disappearance Roger recalled a conversation with Fergie in which he hinted, no averred that someone had forced you to leave us and head up here. The manner of it all caused us to think it likely that those who threatened him may have used similar tactics upon you.

If that is so we are, or Roger is, in a good position to find out more about them and help you to know just why these people would choose to move against you. Speaking for myself, knowing you and all that I have learnt of you, Norman, you have never been at odds with anyone.

We are now helping the police. Well they are helping us! They are in position on the fringe as it were. But very soon, Norman, these people are going to crack. Most of them will be arrested. You and many like you will be understood and cleared. And a peaceful way of life will be restored to all of us at the old palace of justice!'

'Yes indeed. Well, just this Norman, both of us knew we could stake our all that you would never be part of this secret, sick, society as I prefer to think of it. But it may be that you will have learned some small item about the association as a whole, or any individual you know or

43

think to be involved. Any information, however trivial, that anyone of us can supply to the police will hasten the hour when the nightmare for people like Fergie and, I think, yourself will come to an end. The police are eager to come into the picture and make the arrests of which Tony spoke but we know so little. Which is why we do hope that you will be able to help!'

We looked to Norman. He did not speak for what seemed to be a long drawn-out minute. He placed his finger-tips to each temple as if in prayer before turning our way.

He gave a long imploring look towards us which I thought implied an eagerness to deliver up the burden of a secret into safe hands.

He said: 'It is something from which my mind is never free and excessive thought, leads, at times, to confusion. It is then I vacillate between faith in former colleagues and a persistent niggling doubt that maybe any one of them might have been watching and waiting for me to commit that stupid act. As you asked your question I realised that, detached from involvement as you are, one or both of you may see or read into events which I propose to tell you as fully and openly as I know how, any action or intention not as straightforward as it appeared to me at the time. So it may help if I just tell my story and leave you to judge.

You know the circumstance by which I came to be in London without Rene. I recall that even I laughed at the absurdity of it. We were all so sure it was to be of only short duration. At first I lived in what was no more than good clean digs, although the board beside the entrance announced Glenthorne Guest House. It would perhaps have been better had I been in conventional digs. The residents of Glenthorne were largely made up of one night and short stay commercials. Each morning at breakfast, new faces appeared and those who were not reading a newspaper seemed loath to enter into conversation beyond a comment on the weather.

I was homesick and my mood of depression deepened from day to day. I made my first, formal application for transfer back to the area from which I had come. Crown court, Magistrates court, County court, I told them I would serve anywhere within commuting distance from Rene and our home. Had I a law background it would have been oh so easy. But in these days of computers and, with them, centralised management services, vacancies from junior book-keeper to senior accountant are as thick on the ground as duck ponds in the Sahara.

It was then that two juniors in my general office, Mary and Janet, came to ask if I would consider renting a small furnished flat with them on a renewable one year lease. They said it was necessary for an adult in responsible employment, with commensurate salary, to enter into the agreement as lessee. I cannot now remember the name of the owner or how they got to know of its availability. It was like finding gold dust getting the chance of a flat at moderate rental in Central London. A couple taking a fixed term appointment abroad, yes, that I do remember about the owners. Anthony Strickland kindly vetted and O.K'd the agreement for me and I signed. There were those who raised their eyebrows because we all three worked in the same section but apart from giving the girls assurances that I would continue my share of the rent for the first twelve months, come what may, the arrangement was a practical one, beneficial to all three of us.

Both rent and housekeeping bills were shared on a 30/30/40 per cent ratio. I had the benefit of a room to myself, although it was small. The girls did the cooking and, I am ashamed to say, most of the chores. It was working quite well, although after sending my cheque to Rene I was left with very little for leisure and pleasure.

45

Fortunately there was a TV set in the flat and a library close at hand.

Then on two out of three settling up days Janet came to me alone and told me her credit card debts made it impossible for her to chip in her full share. Could she pay half then and make good the arrears by instalments over the ensuing months. She was nineteen and Mary twenty-one and therefore two salary increments behind, whilst still trying to keep pace with Mary in clothes and social activities. They both loved dancing, modern, ballroom and, of course, disco.

On one of the now increasing number of weekends when to save money, I had forgone my visit home to Rene, I had, on the Saturday gone to bed at around midnight, the girls having told me they were going to a gala night disco. I heard them come in but my room was not equipped with a beside lamp and I had no idea of time, neither did I, in my sleepy state, care. I was however, a little nearer wakefulness when my door opened and in complete darkness a whispering Janet commenced to tell me that Mary had picked up with this nice young 'fella', that he had 'had a couple' and did not want to drive his car as there were police all round the dance hall. So he was going to stay with Mary until about six o'clock. I found myself whispering also, but protesting that he could use a chair in the living room when her voice, now close said: 'So I have come to stay with you.' And as she said it she slid silently and effortlessly between the sheets beside me. I continued a form of protest, my voice increasing to near normal volume but I am sure I did not comprehend the words I uttered such was my startled and bemused state. Janet then tenderly took my right hand and every bit as gently placed it upon her naked left breast which was so firm that although she lay flat it was as though moulded upwards to a small hard nipple. As she pressed her fingers to me encouraging a caressing movement I was vitally aware of the breathtaking shapeliness and allure of her body. I let my fingers run from between her breasts down and over the tense flesh of her navel and beyond. Whilst whispering to me on entering the room she had removed every article of her clothing. I am not even remotely suggesting that I was seduced by that young girl. From the very first contact I was the wholehearted prime mover in what, for me, was a pleasing sexual experience.

She was not without knowledge but I cannot, even now believe that her visit to my room and to my bed was in any way premeditated, still less that she would allow herself to be used in something intended to harm me. But she did allow her failure to manage her money to necessitate the now regular appeal to me to accept only a token contribution to the running costs of the flat and the hollow words of intention to repay were no longer made. Because of that night I had always agreed and when I did she would say that she thought of me as a super darling and as I was so very good to her she could cuddle me all night, every night. I met such talk with a frown of annoyance and did not contemplate whether or not I would still desire her. The whole episode was over and had made me even more anxious to rush back to Rene.

My own finances were now in a sorry state. Our joint bank account balance was almost non-existent. I had sold my camera and radio cassette player and made application to take surrender value of my life insurance policy. Don't such things take a hell of a time when you need them most?

I again contacted the head of personnel management and told him that if my transfer was not soon forthcoming I would be forced to leave the department, leave the service, go home and become one of the army of unemployed. Something I was terribly anxious to avoid. I considered going to staff welfare where it is commonplace to tell of

47

ones mounting debts — unless you happen to be a chief accountant with access to quite a lot of money.

Thinking along those lines brought to mind a conversation I had with Grainger about a week earlier. It could be better described as a one-sided conversation that Grainger had with me. He was a member of my staff at the time. The general drift of what he said was that it would be possible for people in my position to remove a sizable sum, put it on short term deposit, take the profit, restore the sum and then repeat the process add infinitum. I did take part sufficiently to reply that we were paid a little more than the mental and physical demands merited adding sarcastically that the amount no doubt included a trustworthyness bonus. I then said that his suggestion would lead to the shortest and quickest route to any prison one cared to name. He appeared to be unconvinced.

I soldiered on looking daily for the envelope that would contain the insurance rebate with which I could buy precious time. Ironically it was from the contents of another envelope that the crunch blow fell upon me. It was from dear Rene. She wrote that she could put what she had to say so much better in a letter: by telephone she would not know how or where to begin. Her mother had suffered early onset of senile dementia, with a gradual decline in her ability to cope. A bout of influenza had brought about a collapse of that ability and she was now a danger to herself. My mind rebelled as my eyes scanned the words line by line. The doctor could have her admitted to a mental home at no expense to anyone except the State. But my Rene's Mum in a mental home! It would kill her and that would kill my Rene. She did not at all times know her daughter but to let her stay in her own home surroundings, with everything she knew close at hand, could maybe hold off for a while the day when she would become a cabbage. Rene, with a heart so much bigger than mine had the answer: she was covering a twelve hour day shift of care and supervision and a night nurse had commenced duties four nights previously. But night nurses don't come cheap.

I read and re-read the letter and stared at the wall in front of me. Worry was gone, hassle was gone, doubt was gone. I knew what I had to do. I went to the office, to my desk, to the safe and made over to myself the sum of five thousand pounds.'

Norman Cartwright had been looking anywhere but at us. Now he gave a challenging stare to each of us in turn.

'Well, that is how I got there,' he said. 'I know that you wish me to tell you about people and their demands; pressures and my break from it all. But it is almost the time at which Rene asked me to stop and get you something to drink before lunch. A bottle of beer or a medium sherry. What is it to be?'

Beer it was for the three of us and a sherry for Rene who joined us as Norman went for the drinks.

Being short tended to emphasise her plumpness as did being viewed together with the six feet slimness of Norman. I put her age at the second half of the forties, his some seven years older. Kindness shone in her face. I could now well understand as I remembered Norman's assertion that her doughty defence of their home had been as much for him as for anything else. Having now met them both I could picture that way of life having as its theme contentment rather than excitement, the tapestry of life preferred to the tinsel. The accountant in Norman had preferred to take promotion for the security the increased pension would later provide. For Rene there would be many more important considerations. She was born to care, he perhaps to worry but both with kindness at heart. In the nicer sense of the phrase, they deserved one another.

At lunch and with the knowledge that Norman had related his narrative, Rene was content to discuss, as we all were, a subject from which there seemed to be no escape. My senses were alerted when Tony said ostensibly to Norman but in the manner of thinking aloud: 'Was a very close friendship or any relationship between Grainger and Janet evident from their behaviour at work?'

Something similar had been coming into my mind and so it was I who replied: 'I get the drift of the question, Tony. You are thinking that Grainger could have been using Janet to push Norman into deeper financial difficulty.'

'Yes, but not necessarily with Janet having knowledge of the part she was playing in the Grainger scheme. Realistically I think not; had he taken her that much into his confidence she would have been in possession of a weapon against him and was not the type to shy from using it to her own advantage. Norman, she is not just the vivacious young spendthrift you think her to be. You are too kindly and generous in your appraisal of the young.'

Rene said: 'You are so right. I have always thought our inability to have children to be the cause of his unfounded faith in each and every one of them. Why! he even thinks that grown-up vice can only begin on becoming adult.'

We grinned and Tony continued: 'Grainger would only have to say to her something like ''a young girl like you should have a Sugar Daddy. Then you would be able to keep up with all the Marys of this world. You are living with one in that flat. Old Cartwright is loaded, he has more money than he needs. Give him a smile and a cuddle, say a few sweet words and he will get you the moon and throw in the stars.'' That I suggest, is how he pointed the way for her to achieve for him what he wanted: your increased impoverishment. She getting what she wanted: you to subsidise her improved standard of dress and social fun. Pointing the way, he appears to be good at it. He pointed the way for you, Norman, although when he did so every instinct within you rejected it. But he hoped and perhaps knew there would be a straw to break the camel. Then you would take his route and take the money.'

Norman's head dropped forward and his shoulders sagged as if in contrite remorse. He muttered as if to himself 'A thief, a criminal.'

'Neither of those things, my friend,' said Tony consolingly. 'You borrowed that money, albeit illegally, but you borrowed it. Now who in the world do you think, when he hears the whole story is going to brand you a criminal?'

Lunch was over and we returned to the lounge. Rene had declined to join us despite our joint remonstrations, and after a meaningful look of relief and gratitude towards Tony, gathered up some dishes and headed for the kitchen saying 'I must be about a woman's work.' I feel sure I detected a misty dampness to her eyes.

Norman told us how after making the money payable to himself, he had banked it and immediately sent a cheque for the full amount to Rene. How all of his nerve ends would not stop jumping, his mouth and throat stop feeling so dry. How he had hunger pains but could not have eaten a thing. That he could neither stand still nor sit still.

He continued: 'The next morning Grainger brought a man to me saying that he was from personnel management and wished to see me privately. I was still in a bit of a state and cannot remember if either of them mentioned a name and it follows that if they did I have forgotten it, as it would appear I have so many things. Of one thing I am certain, I had not seen him before. He told me that a book-keeping discrepancy had come to notice. It was only then that I was consciously aware that Grainger had stayed on. An icy calm came over me as it had when I decided to divert money to my own use. 'I know of the matter to which you refer.' I said 'The discrepancy is factual and I do not challenge your assertion. I shall now go to the chief

51

administrator to give notice of immediate resignation and have no fear, I shall face up to the consequences of my action.' He seemed taken aback and to my surprise I heard Grainger interceding on my behalf. He was saying that such action was surely unnecessary. He said that he knew that I had financial worries. How? I asked myself. He said that he was a member of an association formed to, among other things, arrange relief to honourable men like myself who found themselves in a temporary state of intolerable anxiety. I knew nothing of such things and thought that he was perhaps saying, in effect, that he was a Mason. He asked the man to allow sufficient time for him to make enquiries and arrangements.

Pointing towards me he said: 'This man is ill and could not give a true account of himself to the chief administrator or to anyone.' My agitated state was returning so I was overcome with relief when I heard them agree that I should be taken home, go to bed and return at four o'clock when the man from management would also be there. Mary not Janet was sent for to accompany me, to purchase a sleeping draught and get me to bed, having set an alarm for three o'clock.

I returned at a little after four. Grainger saw me come in, he was alone standing at my desk with a smirk on his face. I have never known him to be with anything other than a smirk on his face. My books were open in front of him. I could not recall giving him my keys to the safe. Do you think that Mary might have taken them for him after I had gone to bed?'

'Very possibly,' I answered, 'but only if she thought it in your best interest, in order that some of your work could be done in your absence, for instance.'

'Yes, I think that too. A good kid young Mary.'

'There you go again, painting them whiter than white but this time there is every reason to suppose that you are right.'

'Grainger reached for the cash book and turned to the previous day, to a money outward payment of five thousand pounds to N. Cartwright, an entry that will haunt me for the rest of my life. Then he flambouyantly flicked over the page to that day's entries and annoyingly tapped his finger on the line of an entry showing five thousand pounds received from N. Cartwright. The anger in my voice must have been obvious as I said: 'You cannot erase one false entry with another.'

'Nothing false about the fifty pound notes, all one hundred of them lying in the cash box in there,' he said, pointing to the safe. 'And there is a cash correction slip initialled N.C.'

'But how — what!' I stammered incredulously.

'My club, my association,' he said, 'They are there to do good works when required. As a member you will decide the rate of repayment and there is no interest charge whatsoever.'

'I am amazed. I have to let it sink in and reflect on possible consequences both here and up at personnel management but my present reaction is one of relief and gratitude. What else is there about your club?'

'Well, it is more of an association, called The New Citizens League. They are going to be big in the future. You really must join.'

'No, not join,' I replied. 'I really am grateful as I said but join, no. I am a bit of an introvert. I play nothing, neither indoors or outdoors. I am completely without talent and a very poor conversationalist. If I ever did entertain the idea I would have to know all about it from A to Z before putting my head inside the door. So can we leave it at that and I will make the repayments through you.'

'Whatever you say, but I think you will regret it when you realise what they can do.' And with that he left me.

The trouble was, I had never liked the man. He was a person with whom I worked, he could never be anything more.

Just three days later I was working at my desk when the door opened and I saw Grainger pointing me out to a man who had now appeared in the doorway beside him. No introduction on this occasion either. Grainger turned and went as the stranger walked over to me. Watching him do so I experienced flashes of recollection. We had met or almost met previously. It was at the Palace garden party two years before, and he had been a member of a party of six or seven of whom I knew just two. He and I had not exchanged a single word, just a polite nod of greeting. As we broke up to continue our gyrations of intermingling before the advent of the Royals, someone, referring to this man and without giving him a name, had mentioned under-secretary and either Home Office or Foreign Office. And now he was close enough to look me directly in the eye without showing the slightest hint of recognition. Even as he was opening with: 'Mr Cartwright I believe,' I was resolving that I too would play the opening round ca' canny and probably for no other reason than that he gave every appearance of doing the same. Still no revelation of his name as he continued: 'Mr Grainger informs me that you are satisfied with the help that we in the New Citizens have been able so far to extend to you. The purpose of my visit, however, is to explore the possibility of further help from us to you and to encourage help or assistance by and from you, to our cause. Monetary contributions are not necessary but canvassing and what I like to call PR work, on the otherhand, are invaluable.'

I said in obvious exasperation: 'I told Grainger that I have no wish to join. That, on the contrary, I have a positive determination not to do so. I shall repay the advance shortly. Within a few days I shall receive a large repayment from an insurance policy when I intend to discharge my indebtedness to you forthwith.'

Both the look on his face and tenor of speech showed a marked tendency towards aggression as he said: 'I was not aware that you possessed sufficient means when the application was made for money that could have been allocated more profitably elsewhere. You will, though, want to carry out a few duties along the lines I have indicated, to record appreciation for the discretion shown at the time of your recent adversity.'

To which I answered: 'I told Grainger at the time that I was extremely grateful for the loan and I remain so today. What are the full nature of the tasks. Provided they do no harm or offend my scruples I am willing to carry out one or two, commensurate with the advance of a very short term loan.'

Now the gloves were off. Anger welled up in his face and a look of dislike showed in his eyes. 'Scruples! You talk of scruples!' he said. 'Start thinking of performing tasks commensurate with avoiding imprisonment, followed by a life close to the gutter. You will work to assist our campaign against those of the left who advocate even anarchy to seize power and you will influence the media with the weight of canvassed petitions of the need for firmer, stronger and tougher government.'

The enormity of the potential power he wielded over me served to bring from within me the same ice cool reasoning capability that had come to my aid twice before in the recent traumatic days. I firmly, and now quite loudly, told him that our meeting was at an end and unless he left the building immediately I would have the security staff detain him and press charges. The effect was dramatic to say the least. Not a word of any dire fate that would be brought to my door. Walking from my room to the corridor I watched him leave by means of swift measured footsteps.

I am only sorry that I failed to get his name but if, as I think, he is from within the service he should be quite easily traced and I can identify him. Of course Grainger may well have a change of heart and be willing, perhaps anxious, to name him.

The secretary to the head of department was kindly instrumental in obtaining for me an almost immediate interview with her boss to whom I fully confessed my acts of folly. He was most understanding and, although I have to attend before a disciplinary tribunal later this year, he is going to do all in his power to mitigate the outcome. I am suspended on pay until that time. And there you have the full account of my disappearance from the courts.'

We said our goodbyes over a hurried early tea. Hurried and early so that the helicopter could make the South Bank heliport before dusk, thus freeing the Inspector pilot and his operator to make an early return to base. The short journey to Tony's home was made by taxi. Carol was not yet there. Neither of us had really expected that she would be.

We took a can of beer apiece from the fridge and without so saying knew that we both wished to discuss assumptions and implications to be drawn from all that we had heard.

I said: 'Whilst I acknowledge the very serious threat of the pressures placed upon Norman, and we must be right to assume also on Fergie, I nevertheless get no feeling of volume sufficient to warrant being described as a sinister threat. I would not attempt to write it off as the action of a gang of bored and empty headed youngsters, nor can I bless it with the respectability and rectitude I understand to be associated with the concerted actions of Freemasons. No, I think I go for a small objectionable and quite cranky political pressure group.'

'Political — yes, pressure group, maybe yes,' Tony replied. 'But on your sense of volume point: if we increase

56

the volume, at what stage can we declare it to be sinister? Of the attempted coercions, we now know of Norman and Fergie just within our close associates. Thinking in terms of the whole country it would be easy to accept a multiplication of one hundred and not too difficult to allow for a growing increase to one thousand. Now does the situation take on a sinister aspect? The Masterson mob we have, in my opinion, correctly deduced to be the heavy squad keeping inquisitive eyes and minds at a lot more than arms length. And keeping the finances of the league, or whatever they choose to call themselves, very much in the black by means of hijacks, hold ups and the like. Apply our multiplication ratio and what have we got?

Then we have Grainger and the, so far, unnamed visitors, enthusiastic volunteers I will label them. Perfectly possible for there to be pockets in every city, town and hamlet. Add the categories together and you have an inordinately dangerous organisation which, while not necessarily formed for evil, is certainly not good for the rest of us.'

'Wow! Once again I say thank heavens you are on my team. Your ability to assess situations in a matter of moments is similar to that of Helen Mandrake. She has a brilliant mind, is capable of unravelling knotty problems at speed, can see through a verbal smoke screen as it is being laid and can plan, and create rules and guide-lines for the administration of a plan off the top of her head.'

'The lady has certainly swept you overboard,' laughed Tony. 'But my effort was mere conjecture and influenced by what my father said about police undercover reports bearing a proximity to our findings.'

'How about Grainger,' I ventured. 'If we can encourage the police to take him into protective custody away from the others it is my guess that he will sing like a canary.'

'That is a good enough guess to be a certainty.'

8

There can surely be nothing quite like new love to create a feeling of joy and eager expectancy about a return to duty, even on a Monday morning, especially when the object of one's affection works in the same establishment. I had received encouraging signs that maybe my love for the lady might be returned. And what a bonus to have the approval of the Lord Chancellor together with his personal directive that we keep company on all suitable occasions. Just thinking of Helen I knew that all such occasions would be entirely suitable.

I felt a measure of concern at the love at first sight effect that Helen held for me from the very start. I had trodden the road to romance before and at the point of failure then, had I not wished to hell that the affair had never begun? But Helen appeared to wield power and authority with a charisma and charm that drew all to her. I so admired her intellect and qualities that rendered her a power for good. I was fascinated but refused to admit infatuation.

But first things first. I had hardly set foot in my room when the telephone rang, it was the attendant at the main entrance to say:

'I have a gentleman here Sir. Says he has come by arrangement to explain the changes in your insurance.'

I could almost feel the smile play around my lips as I answered:

'Fine.'

'So you'll be down?'

'Yes, right away.'

I saw him as I neared the security check points and yes,

he was wearing a pin-striped suit! He was tall and there the resemblance to most people's idea of how a policeman should look ended. Slim and over neatly dressed in up to the minute business fashion, it was as though he wished to draw attention to himself in order to be accepted and thus overlooked.

As we shook hands and he introduced himself as Johnny Cousens I looked closely into his face and thought that perhaps, just perhaps, the glass in those spectacles had been prepared without having to conform to a prescription. We agreed the Alexander in Carnaby Street to be our meeting place, the milling shoppers and sightseers excellent cover for two men having a beer and talking for only as long as it takes for an exchange of information.

He then told me that the police would be shadowing the security van when it left Mastersons using a number of unmarked vehicles, all with their individual looking car radios tuned to just one transmitter. He said that one or two of them had a bit of a banger appearance but with an engine under the bonnet that could hold its own with anything on the road. The police felt sure that the journey would be made before the ninth. One reason being that the ninth was a Saturday and the users would prefer the anonymity of one among many similar vehicles on a Monday to Friday road. The observations on Mastersons had commenced two days previously, shortly after our conversation with Sir John at Guildford, and we were asked to stay away.

As briefly as possible I recounted the visit to Cartwright. He listened, I thought quite inattentively, casually looking at Portraits on the wall, at people passing, at anything but me, the speaker. Not a bit like my image of the note book and pencil and 'Anything you say'. He seemed to read my mind and smiling, made a deliberately obvious motion of switching off a small tape recorder in his pocket. It was then that he seriously cautioned that no word of the visit to Cartwright should pass to anyone else. He feared that if news of it reached certain ears the Cartwrights would be subjected to reprisal, if only to warn Tony and I not to meddle.

He gave me a telephone number saying that it was ansaphone equipped avoiding the necessity for me to identify myself to anyone but him.

'Just record the message, I will know that it is from you.' He reminded me that he had no intention of using my place of work to make further contacts but would not hesitate to do so in a situation of urgency.

As he left I decided to use Lord Garlands licence to roam as an invitation to seek out Helen. With Johnny Cousens words still fresh in my ears I decided that if asked about my weekend I would say that it consisted of a little flying and catching up on overdue visiting.

Helen was not in her room but a young girl seated there kindly told me that she intended to visit the law library and could well be there. As I made my way to the Queens building in which that library is housed, I pondered my puzzlement as to how this woman, who from our first meeting impressed me greatly, could have remained unnoticed before. She surely could not have held her senior position very long or I would have known. An answer was forthcoming in less than one minute when, at the front entrance to the building, I met John Hancock, a Chancery Division colleague. John gave me an extremely quizzical look when, in reply to my question 'What do you know of Miss Helen Mandrake?' he said:

'You have the advantage of me in that I have not met the lady and, for all I know, I have not set eyes on her. But that is hardly surprising in an organisation as large as this in which total staff numbers are recorded in thousands. It is, however, my understanding that she was head-hunted from within the private sector and that the Lord Chancellor has claimed her recruitment and subsequent success to be an indication of his ability to pick a winner.

I took the lift to the library, passing a conference room on the way. As I stepped from the lift a door opened and I heard a voice, the voice, the tannoy voice mentally transporting me back to Fergie's room and to that evening. There was no doubt in my mind. I could not mistake it then or ever. I pulled back to the already closed doors of the lift and by inclining my head I could see and hear that the voice belonged to a man with his back to me, holding the handle of the open door while speaking into the room. All I heard was:

'It must be done tonight and the timing has to be exact. Boulting must be warned to stay sober and start moving the consignment into his cabin on the strip. Mills and Korff must be on the ball for the switch. I will go myself, there is a good train from Waterloo at six-nine and another at six-fifty, I shall try for the first. If you need to contact me I will be in my office until five-thirty.'

As the door closed I stepped out to pass him on the corridor rather than skulk at the lift entrance. Five feet nine or ten, stocky build, dark hair, quite an ordinary face with a close trimmed moustache.

He made no sign of recognising me as I moved slightly aside to allow him to pass unhindered. But I had recognised him, having seen his photograph in a newspaper within the past few days. Somebody Townsend founder of a new pressure group to obtain tax incentives for exporters. A small success and I bounded jauntily along the rest of the way to the library, but would have dearly loved to get a look at the faces of those still in the conference room. You can't win 'em all I told myself, well not all at once.

Helen was not in the library. As I made to leave I saw

on the notice board a schedule of reservations for meetings in the conference room. There was no entry for that morning. I descended in the lift to the hall where I saw Helen talking to a couple, whom I judged to be litigants waiting for their case to be called. As I approached she looked my way and turned from them to me. A brief greeting and I began to tell her of my encounter near the conference room and how I had wished to meet her at that time so that we might have kept a casual watch at each end of the corridor to get a good look at whoever left that room. I enjoyed telling her of the events and she seemed to regard me with a new respect. She said how great it would be working together. We were now really a team I thought. I repeated the Waterloo train times and said:

'As it is out of office hours I will cover it myself and report the result tomorrow.'

She smiled, coyly for someone of her self assurance, and said: 'You don't get rid of me that easily my friend, you will need me and who knows where the journey might take us!'

Nothing appropriate would spring to mind so I just grinned. When I told her the conference room meeting was not on the schedule she said: 'It was not an official meeting, just a little staff association pow-wow. I think I may have approved it myself.'

'What about Townsend, though?'

'People from the private sector are often invited,' she shot back, with a touch of mild sarcasm, 'to discuss, among other things, salary and wage differentials.'

We travelled together by bus. Strand, Waterloo Bridge and no sooner on than off. It was three minutes to six as we walked onto the concourse. I caught sight of him looking up at the indicator board. Recognition no doubt showed in my face and Helen had a look of expectation as I said: 'There he is, next to the lady in the red coat.'

'I see him, the one with the weekend bag.'

'Yep, except that the weekend is over.'

'Fool. Will you get the tickets while I see what he does. The first stop appears to be Woking so if we have tickets to there we can pay excess should we have to go on.'

The platform number had still not been signalled as I returned with the tickets to see the darling standing within three feet of Townsend, Colin Townsend, as I now recalled. It was as though she just had to be at arms length in case he made a dash for it. I put it down to the fact that when young we chaps fantasised being Sherlock Holmes or Hercule Poirot and knew just how to stalk ones prey without a chance of being detected. Whereas for the little charmers it was Joan of Arc or Florence Nightingale. Very laudable but useless when it comes to suppression of crime.

As I drew near the platform number flicked over and we all made our way to number eight. Moving away I noticed the names commenced to flick over on another column and on stopping gave details of the six-fifty or eighteen-fifty as it should better be known. It too was to have a first stop at Woking then on to Basingstoke, Southampton and Bournemouth. The one we were about to board was to call at Woking, Guildford, Haselmere and Portsmouth. So — if either train was suitable for him then Woking must be his destination.

Helen and I sat at one end of the compartment in which Townsend was already seated at the other. I had obtained first class tickets to cover the eventuality. It would seem that he was watching the pennies. I told Helen of my observation at the board and its pointer to Woking.

She raised her eyebrows high to give a wide eyed look and said: 'O.K. sleuth, I'll come quietly.'

As the train slowed in its approach to Woking station we unobtrusively prepared for a swift exit but Townsend just sat there. Sherlock Holmes within me was a little lost as how to cope if he made a dash as the guard's whistle sounded the off. But no, he still sat there with every appearance of being quite unperturbed. We headed on to Guildford.

And at Guildford he left no doubt as to his intention. He stood up well in time and slowly gathered his case, his mackintosh, brolly and even his newspaper and made for the exit passage with its connecting exit door. We were handicapped right from the start. A lady, together with her suitcase, was in the little passage at our end and stood between me and the door. I said to Helen: 'The footbridge, but fast. I will cover the subway. Keep well up in case he diverts onto one of the other platforms to lay up until we have all left.' By then I was onto the platform having lifted down the lady's case as I went. People were descending from what appeared to be every door, standing to look about them whilst deciding which way to move off. I thought I saw his head and shoulders among a number of people, all of whom were between the subway, the entrance to which I was approaching and the footbridge further on. I had another sighting, more than halfway down the slope of the subway. I found myself mentally urging Helen to speed it to the stairs as I became more despondent that the man ahead of me was Townsend.

'Roger, Roger, Roger Diamond,' I heard Helen's voice behind me.

I turned to see her side stepping and pushing her way towards me. 'The stairs Helen,' I seemed to almost whine as if in defeat, 'he is on the footbridge and could be anywhere shortly.'

'He is not,' she answered, somewhat brusquely still moving forward, 'he is ahead and has turned right at the bottom heading for number two platform, which leads to the main booking hall and onto the street.

I knew that my number-one hunch could have been

anywhere by then and tried to catch some of her enthusiasm that the man ahead was indeed Townsend. Neither of us spoke concentrating as we were on moving faster than those around us. When we reached the barrier the ticket collector was asking for his pound of flesh, or more precisely the difference in fare between Woking and Guildford. I left Helen to fix it and ran across the hall after the man going out through the swing doors. As I got to the doors, he was heading for the taxi rank. I spurted a little more and drew level. It was not Colin Townsend. As I returned, dejected, to Helen and the ticket collector I noticed a train in on platform number five.

'Which one is that?' I asked.

'The Woking and Waterloo fast,' he said, looking at his watch, 'due out now.' My legs jerked forward automatically but even as they did so the train pulled away from the platform and away from Guildford.

'God, he really has beaten us,' I blurted out, 'he will be in time to join the six-fifty from Waterloo and make for any place of his choice on the Bournemouth line.'

Helen was devastated. 'I gaffed, I blew it,' she repeated again and again. 'Our first real joint venture and I pull a boner. What must you think of me?'

'Well, as one who from the very first has voted you brain of Britain, who acknowledges you to be the fastest ever at sizing up a situation and taking control — I think you fell flat on your face.' I grinned and holding her arm added: 'Now does that console you?'

'Yes thank you, you are most kind. Now I have thought of a consolation for both of us. The conversation you heard at the conference room door has supplied a couple of clues, very very remote but nevertheless I am sure you were right and he has headed down the line. I propose that we take some Garland leave-of-absence and tomorrow set out with an over night bag or preferably over two-night bag, and try to find where Townsend went and why.' Looking at me with a slight, short-lived, lowering of her eye lashes she added:

'Now, does that console you?'

How could I ever ask for more? A tiny acknowledgement that I held a place, however small, but a place in her thinking and the utter failure of the evening was removed at a stroke.

A train to get home by seemed the next item for consideration but as Woking and Waterloo came to mind thoughts on the earlier problem returned.

'It has to be Woking, Helen. Only with Woking as his destination could he be equally content with the six-nine and the six-fifty. Tonight's little episode was just lack of concentration. He failed to get off at Woking, corrected the error at Guildford and has returned to Woking. The place he intended to reach all along. Avoiding people was furthermost from his thoughts allowing him to be blissfully unaware of our prancing around trying to keep up with him.'

'I have to agree that as a probable explanation. Does that mean our mini-holiday has to be spent in Woking?'. There should be a pat answer to that which would not give offence to anyone other than a handful of residents of that town or to supporters of its football team. I could not think of one however, because, smitten by one of my hunches I went to the booking office grille and purchased a current timetable for the region. 'This will reveal all if there is anything to reveal,' I said to Helen.

'Here we are, Mondays to Fridays, Waterloo to Basingstoke and beyond, 18-09 stopping at Surbiton, Woking, Basingstoke, Winchester, Eastleigh, Southampton, Bournemouth and then all stations to Weymouth. Next we have the 18-50 stopping at Woking, Basingstoke, Southampton and Bournemouth. In another section we find 18-09 Waterloo to Guildford and beyond stopping at Woking, Guildford, Haselmere and Portsmouth. So you see there are two 18-09 trains. The fast one gets cracking to a first stop at Woking. The other sets off in the slower lane and makes a stop at Surbiton before the one at Woking. The first, the one we were on, branches off to Guildford and the now slightly later one carries on down the Bournemouth line just that bit ahead of the 18-50, travelling the same route. Of course I cannot be sure without checking but I'll wager that it goes very much like that. What do you think?'

'Amazed, impressed and yes, I think that you are right.'

'Which means that Townsend did knowingly do a doubling back avoidance tactic and, what is far more serious, he knew before he came to Waterloo that he was to be followed. That puts the mini-holiday back to square one, as outlined by you.' I paused to smile. 'But unless Townsend is used to being followed and has a contingency plan for every journey, we have a leak in the plumbing. The young girl I saw in your room this morning, is she reliable?'

'I would hope so. I am not the recruitment officer but when they are sent to someone like myself, with the nature of the work I am doing, they should be water tight.'

When I asked her if the girl would have known that she and I had been out together and if Waterloo station could have been mentioned she said:

'I don't know but quite possibly. Lord Garland had decided that you and I should be seen together as close friends. If she had asked me I would have told her. Damn it, she has surely been screened and passed as reliable.'

At long last we got a train and at Helen's request parted at Waterloo but not before I had asked if I might pick her up at home in the morning. She said that as she had a

couple of things to do at the courts before leaving, would
I make it there.

9

I decided to walk back to my place. It was a lovely clear
night the weather remarkably mild and I had been happy
to note the forecast said we could expect it to continue so
for some days to come. I had climbed the slope and as I
walked onto Waterloo bridge the fascination of the river
at night gripped me yet again. I never tire of being there.
The reflection of the embankment lights seemingly as deep
set into the water as the actual lamps are above the ground.
A place to paint pictures in the mind, to travel, to swish
away to New York, to Paris, to Sidney, to Rome. The
world is yours and you hold the brush with which to paint
in the scene. Your scene! But the ground is there to speed
back to, to replace one's feet firmly and think of matters
of real concern such as being out-manoeuvred by Townsend
and possible sources of the information leaked to him.
Could it be that he and they, whoever 'they' were, were
paying as much attention to Helen and I as we to them.
Just suppose that, despite the dead-pan face, Townsend
had recognised me as we passed and having done so would
he not contemplate the possibility that I had overheard his
conversation. Now to push the quirk of fate a little further
— that he had still been in or around the Queens building
to see Helen and I in animated conversation and after we
had parted followed her to her room. A warm day, a door
ajar and he might well have heard Helen say to her assistant
something like: 'I shall be staying on until five-thirty as
I am going on to Waterloo with Roger Diamond.'
Confirmation easily obtained as I imagined Townsend
calling on Helen's assistant a little later with 'Helen and

Roger are, I think, to meet my wife and I at Waterloo this evening at six. Have I got the right day, do you know?' If my supposition was in anyway correct the Lord Garland 'cover' for Helen and myself was blown and 'they' would no longer be looking at us as just another couple.

As I walked on, thinking ahead to the next two or three days I saw no real possibility of achievement now that we had no idea of Townsend's whereabouts and without him to lead us to the area where one or two clues I had gleaned from his conversation might have been of use. Helen now thought of the trip as a consoling cure for despondency after the Guildford station debacle. She had been so stricken with guilt it would have been very much less than kind to deny her the chance to make amends. And let's face it, who in his right mind would spurn an opportunity to escort the beautiful Helen over such a long period?

I had to contact Johnny Cousens to pass on what I thought indicated imminent movement of the security van. I changed route to take me to the law courts where in my room one telephone was on instant direct dialing, a luxury I did not enjoy at the hotel. My earlier resolve on the need for sharper awareness seemed to be going a little over the top when I began to sense that the fellow four yards behind had been there for quite a while. I stopped to look into a window and he stopped to adjust his shoe lace. So, I crossed to the other side of the Strand while he kept right on course and I felt quite a fool.

I was admitted to the building and moving along the dark corridors to my room I considered the news report to be dictated to the ansaphone as it was now past one o'clock in the morning. After the briefest moment of recording noise there was a click and on came the voice of Johnny Cousens, bright as a button and seemingly pleased to talk with me. I told him of the conversation I had overheard and after I had asked him if he agreed that

70

it suggested an early removal of the van, he said:

'It is on its way, Roger, left this morning and at the moment is in a large dockside vehicle park in Southampton where we expect it to remain until later this morning. We believe that there is one person still on board but cannot be sure as we are keeping distance observation only. It seems to confirm the link with your man Towsend and the beyond Woking theory that you have so studiously worked on.'

'Thank-you Johnny and thank you for the Roger. I have been unaware of how to address you by rank, Inspector or Sergeant?'

Quietly and oh so modestly the words came back:

'Superintendent actually. I was lucky enough to qualify for advanced promotion entry but, providing you do not mind, I do prefer Johnny.'

'How to win friends and influence people,' I silently chided myself.

Reminding him of my proposed trip with Helen I added that I accepted all that he had just told me as for my ears only.

He replied: 'Thanks, and have a good trip, I never seem to get those conditions imposed on me when keeping observation. Do try to telephone me between seven and ten tomorrow evening. I shall make myself available here and should be in a position to update you on the location of the van.'

'Thanks and goodnight — well good morning.'

When I put down the telephone I found myself saying 'What an extremely pleasant man.'

It was nearly two am when I came out from the front of the building and made my way to the rear and on to Lincoln's Inn Fields. I crossed by the diagonal pathway and as I got to the one light at the centre I became aware that a man was overtaking me.

As he drew level he glanced in my direction and in a quiet well spoken voice said: 'Do not get involved in something you cannot handle.'

It was the man I had seen in the Strand earlier.

He had waited until we were into the lamplight to ensure that I would see that what his fingers were toying with was a flick-knife. The degree to which I might possess bravery had never been tested and I hoped that this would not be the first time. In his other hand he held two playing cards. I could not see which cards they were but he said: 'The Jack of Diamonds — that's you, can easily meet The Ace of Spades — that's death. Cut it out, as of now or the cards will come together.'

With more play of his fingers upon the knife he backed away, left the path and moved swiftly across the grass and into the darkness.

My first reaction once he had gone was a desire to laugh. A psychiatrist would no doubt tell me that laughter, or in my case the desire to laugh, would have been prompted by relief at not coming into closer contact with the flick-knife. But at the time, it was the amateur theatrical performance of a truly ham actor. At that hour of the morning a stimulant would have been essential to put dramatic menace into such corny lines and in his case I thought drugs rather than alcohol. I wondered what form of coercion had been used to make him carry out this repayment duty for the New Citzens League.

I felt convinced that for the present no physical harm was intended, for had it been I would be lying injured or dead. It was a warning, a message, food for thought in which I was already actively engaged. I was somewhat in awe at the speed with which they had mounted the action to scare me off. This man had doubtless remained continuously within visible distance of Helen and I from six o'clock at Waterloo or before without arousing the merest suggestion of awareness in either of us. Our attention had, of course, been very much concentrated on Townsend. However it had been delivered, it was an aggressively strong warning and the threat could not be dismissed lightly.

Could Helen have been subjected to a similar experience on her way home? I realised that I had no idea where she lived. I determined to insist that she drop out of this now deadly serious game of cops and robbers. I thought that they might more easily have achieved their goal, as far as I was concerned, if a threat to harm Helen had been made.

As I reached my hotel the hands of my watch confirmed that it was ten minutes after three o'clock. To contact Johnny Cousens again, early in the morning was a must; so three and a half hours sleep was the maximum for which I could hope and I knew that I would not be a creature of sweetness and light.

My friend, the Superintendent, answered his telephone promptly. For one who had been in conversation with me at around two am he sounded very full of life. A state that I was finding difficult to approximate and certainly could not match. As a prelude to recounting the happenings since that early conversation I acknowledged that what I had to tell him reduced my potential as an undercover man to just about zero, but that I would nevertheless like to continue in whatever role he felt might be useful.

When I had brought him up to date with the whole of my report he said:

'Roger, if speaking to one of my men, I would now be saying the risks are minimal and mean just that, I assure you. But you are an ordinary citizen carrying out a citizens responsibility in an extraordinary and wholly praiseworthy way. You are not expected to take risks, however minimal. No-one is going to express even surprise if you pull out now. In that event we would come in. Lord Garland would feel compelled to call us in. Were he not to we would overrule him and close in on the matters that your efforts have revealed. This is where I begin to twist your arm Roger, my friend. We could not hope to be fully successful if we took over now. Some fish, and unfortunately most of the big ones, would escape the net. On the other hand, should you stay, you could draw their attention and run any red herring trips they care to set whilst we ask your friend Tony who, as you know, has been having a quiet time, to take on the observation with whatever cover you and we can give. It might be prudent if you do not mention this new arrangement to his lordship or he may wonder just who is running his department. Play it cool and cautious, anything not quite so-so, dial for help. I will have this telephone pad monitored continuously and we'll come arunning. Unless you have anything more I will let you go. Goodbye and God bless.

10

After meeting Helen I experienced an increasing sense of relief as first six, then seven minutes passed without mention of a threat having been made to her. So I told her of my light entertainment in the early hours at which she became noticeably distressed saying:

'Roger that is terrible. You must do as he says and stop. I mean it Roger, I really do. I will tell Lord Garland we are unlikely to achieve results and are asking to be allowed to return to normal duties. I will find out if he can see me this morning.'

'Hold on, hold on,' I said firmly. 'The moment you do he will have no option other than to call in the police. That might be for the best but both you and particularly he were very keen to spare the department the trauma of colleague watching colleague.'

Again a complete change of attitude: 'Gosh, you are so right, how could I have so disrgarded our commitment to his lordship's idea. Of course we must get to the bottom of it without it becoming official. But Roger, I have not been threatened, maybe not even suspected. I will do the trailing and listening and then talk over the results with you. Your reasoning is so much more sound and you will still have your part in the joint venture.'

'Reverse the roles, partner and you have just outlined my plan. You to revert to normal working activity but with eyes and ears very much at the alert while I continue to snoop around uninhibited by thoughts of possibly leading you into danger.'

Her smile, I thought, an acknowledgement of my

predictability as she said 'Are we not both saying that we are each unscared by the message, well not sufficiently scared to give up trying, in fact that we shall very shortly be on our little working holiday to heaven knows where.'

'Southampton actually.'

'Southampton!' She placed so much emphasis on the name one might have been forgiven for picturing it as the last place God made. 'Why Southampton?'

With the spectre of Johnny Cousens, with raised cautionary finger, coming into mental vision I said:

'I have this nagging hunch that Townsend is at least that far and most probably a little beyond.'

For a tiny moment she looked surprised. 'Nonsense Roger, absolute rubbish. We were agreed last evening that it just had to be Woking.'

'Whatever happened to the soundness of my reasoning you saw fit to praise just a few moments ago?' I teased. 'From the moment we found there to be a second six-nine train, the longer distance became the more likely.'

We were almost to my car when she said: 'Bournemouth, let's make it Bournemouth, if only because it is a nice place for us to be when we draw a blank. And the choice of hotels is greater.'

As I placed our luggage into the boot I said: 'Greater number, yes and each one to be checked by phone or eliminated by reasoning in our search for Colin Townsend.'

'And repeat it all the way back along the railway possibilities until we find him at Woking,' were her last words as I started the car and moved off.

We booked in at Tree Tops, one of the well appointed independents. If it did lose anything to nationals and multi-nationals in cost cutting efficiency it more than made up in charming personal service. When I asked if Colin Townsend was staying with them, a cursory referral before the never-in-doubt answer 'No Sir'.

My request as to how he would prefer to record our telephone calls was answered with:

'We make no charge for local calls Sir, all other calls will be recorded and included in your bill'.

I went on to explain our desire to trace Townsend whom we thought to be in the area and that might result in many local calls.

Nothing was going to dim the Tree Tops service and he said: 'No matter Sir. If your friend is in Bournemouth he will be staying at one of the local association hotels,' and turning to a girl seated at the end of the reception area, 'Mary have a fax message sent to those so equipped and contact the others yourself asking if a Mr Colin Townsend is staying with them.'

'But that is a mammoth task,' I mildly protested.

With a deft movement of his head towards Mary he quietly said: 'The young lady Sir, perhaps a few chocolates.'

As I mentioned, it was a charming place at which to be staying. Lunch was being served until two-thirty and we entered the dining room well within time.

With Mary making our enquiries and the emphasis now switched to holiday rather than working-holiday, Helen and I walked gently down the pretty winding path, on through the gardens to the sea front. It was mild, the sun shone and only a light breeze rustled the leaves as we made our way to purchase the chocolates for Mary. Later it was delightful to have tea al fresco.

As late afternoon became early evening I had a shower and changed into my lounge suit. With Helen only just preparing her bath I went down to the hall and used a pay phone to speak to Johnny Cousens. He was so very surprised but nevertheless delighted to hear that Helen and I were still in harness as a team. I asked him rightaway if I should in fairness be taking Helen a little more into my confidence, particularly with regard to the van as there appeared to be a connection between Townsend and the van.

'Exactly,' he answered, 'but we can surmise their assumption that your overhearing Townsend's conversation to be the only breach of their security. Knowledge of the van and its contents would have much more serious implications for them. In the interest of her safety as much as anything I want to stress that an odd word or half sentence could indicate knowledge and Roger, what she does not know she cannot be tricked into revealing. Now the van, it passed where you tell me you are, followed the road through Poole and at Wareham turned for Swanage instead of heading on towards Weymouth. And then believe it or not, we the police, lost it, near Corfe Castle. Even as I speak I can almost hear you champing at the bit to get in and tell me that what you heard Townsend say must have been Mills at Corfe, and not Mills and Korff, and so it now reads Mills at Corfe Castle must be on the ball for the switch. We have a host of men looking for the damn thing but should you be able to get down there you are the only one on our side who could instantly recognise him, if he is, as I think he probably is, beavering away at the point of disappearance. Now, after that, we all need to hear something encouraging and I have just that for you. I passed on to the powers that be your suggestion, that if in custody Grainger would tell all or most of what his criminal mind has been able to assimilate. It took only two days of observation to nab him for handling drugs but in a very minor way as he is quite often tempted to do when short of cash. Although his knowledge of the people who comprise the New Citizens League is almost negligible he is, as you forecast, telling us quite a lot about its operation. Take care. Same time tomorrow.'

After calling at reception to be told that Mary's comprehensive efforts had failed to produce news of Townsend, I went to our room where Helen was putting down the telephone at the end of a call to London to, as she said, check on a couple of outstanding matters in her office. She was groomed for the evening and shortly we went down to the bar prior to entering the dining room.

Over dinner I once again raised the question of what to do about Townsend and suggested a run in the car to Poole, Swanage or even down to Weymouth, to enquire at likely hotels before he had a chance to get away. It led to a lively discussion.

'Before a chance to get away,' mocked Helen, 'he has already got away. I knew that before we set off. To be here in Bournemouth is very pleasant, our chance to get over the Guildford gaffe, to restore and renew our friendly feeling for one another. To go chasing along dark strange roads looking for a needle in a haystack is just plain stupid. It will achieve nothing. There is a romantic little playlet on the tele in our room, my vote is for that.'

Without the Johnny Cousens argument, which I could not put, I felt that I had no case at all.

After the mini-play and the news I went to the bathroom to change into shorties. I purposefully lingered and whilst there recalled one or two memorable moments from earlier in the day. The wedding ring she had produced, far too new in condition and design to have been her mothers. Purchased, I fancy, during one of our stops along the way. Our decision to register as Mr and Mrs would hinder persons seeking to trace us. Her choice of Garland as our assumed name had brought happy laughter and light relief to us both.

Coming from the bathroom and bound for the wardrobe I caught sight of her standing at the doors leading onto a tiny balcony, no deeper than the width of one of the doors. One door was in fact slightly ajar. It was still mild with a bright moon in a clear sky and only a gentle breeze moved the air. Clothed in only a silk neglige which the breeze lightly held to the shape of her body, she stood there holding a posture reminiscent of that at our first meeting her head tossed a little high, her hair brushed loose and caressed by the breeze. It was as though she sought inspiration. Perhaps not a goddess but, in my book, as close as a mere mortal could hope to emulate.

At first she seemed completely unaware of my presence, then as in a dream stepping from the past into the present she moved from the balcony into the room. She came to me and lightly took my wrists with her hands.

'You are a good man Roger Diamond, too good, and as she said it she drew my arms to enfold her, stretched up to the tips of her toes and pressed her warm lips upon mine. The urgency that was within her now transmitted to me, we led one another to the bed.

Desires within me to kiss, caress and pet were gently but firmly resisted as she motioned me closer within her. It was as though she had nothing of herself she wished to give me. She had taken to herself a man. Her head still on the pillow, her face moving from side to side revealed a look of anguish tempered with ecstacy. As she became more emotionally stirred her hands with those long fingers, rested on my buttocks. At the moment of climax the fingers were drawn up and back, the finger-nails dug into my skin and cat-like she fiercely drew her hands up over my flesh, letting out a suppressed yell: 'Bleed you bastard, bleed.'

Her body immediately became convulsed with uncontrollable sobbing. Experiencing a mixture of anger, shock and daze I moved aside, lying on my stomach, certain that there would be blood upon my skin. My hand and arm, reaching out to console, was pushed away. The sobbing gradually abated and finally she was quiet and still. I lay thinking, asking myself what sort of man I was. Why had I not retaliated, violence for violence? And then why had I not taken her firmly in my arms and continued so until she was convinced that I would be there until her troubles had passed? I had been too concerned with what had happened to me and not nearly enough with what was happening to her. Convinced that sleep was what she most needed then, I lay very quiet, so quiet that it was I who fell into deep sleep.

I awoke to find that moonlight had given way to sunlight. Helen was nowhere to be seen. The bathroom door was wide open. It was then I saw the sheet of notepaper upon the cabinet beside the bed and on it 'Sorry about the hols. Sorry about everything. H.'. A call to reception and the voice confirmed with, 'Yes, madam had gone'. They had obtained a taxi-cab for her and she left for the station intending to catch the 7-15 am train for London.

I was not finding decision making all that easy. Finally, deciding that a pause to heal, between Helen and myself was desirable, bearing in mind her state of distress and my tender rump, a telephone call later would be more constructive. So I would drive to Corfe Castle to pick up whatever might be left of the trail.

I went to the bathroom for the necessary ablusions and later, ready for breakfast and the outside world I opened the door to the corridor where not far away I saw the room maid with her trolly of bed linen. Beckoning her to the room I showed her the small amount of blood-marking on one of the bed sheets and asked if the cost could be assessed and added to my bill. She was not sure. Perhaps the housekeeper would know. We found that lady at the very large linen cupboards. No there would be no charge, accidents will happen and there are washing powders that remove such stains without leaving a trace. Leaving them together I imagined a likely conversation between them to be 'whatever did the brute do to ladylike Mrs Garland causing her to leave so early and so hastily'.

Before leaving the hotel I returned to our room, not to hunt for a pair of socks or a tie but to look again at the tiny balcony, the french doors, the bathroom and to the now unromantically stripped bed. To where I had experienced a few of what I imagine to be, the many strands of character that make up the remarkable Helen Mandrake.

11

Driving out and away from Bournemouth and heading in the direction of Poole and then on to Swanage, my mind was absorbed with two conflicting trains of thought. Superintendent Johnny Cousens featured in both. His often expressed, though undeserved, faith in my ability to play a larger role in these matters than I would have chosen for myself was to an extent, responsible for my chasing whereever and seeking whatever might be revealed. More importantly I was beginning to like what I was doing. But the continuing gag that Johnny had imposed on me was the cause of friction, however slight, coming between Helen and myself, particularly the misunderstanding at dinner the previous evening. How could she consider other than stupid a suggestion to chase out into the darkness seeking one man, last seen in Guildford. Had I taken her into my confidence with regard to the security van we might in unison, have travelled the road I was presently on. Our impromptu coming together in our room at the hotel might then have been delayed rather than the depressing failure we were both now regretting.

Through Wareham and beyond I came to a point where the road turned right through a full ninety degrees and after a further one hundred and fifty yards, a left turn similarly acute. A narrow secondary road continued the line that the main road had held before the sharp left hand turn. The direction arrow pointing into that turning, boldly indicated Swanage.

I drove into the narrow road, Clifton Road as I observed it to be. The houses on it and in the few inter-connecting roads were of red brick and probably of the early turn of the century period. It was a small area of not very attractive dwellings.

I did not see a church but there were two corner shops, a general store and a pub no bigger than a medium sized double fronted house. There was no road connection that would bring one back onto the main road south but over to the right Holt's Pond Road provided access and by turning left I could have been speeding back to Wareham, Weymouth, Salisbury, Bristol. Think of a town and the road offered a clear run to get there. Was this then the switch for which Mills was to be alerted.

Returning to Clifton Road where it connects with the A351 I parked near to the junction and made my way on foot along the one hundred or so yards between those two sharply angled turnings. On the first run through in the car I had caught a brief glimpse of high double doors. Looking again, and more closely, I noticed that at the top floor and just below the roof there was a hoist arm with pully fitment immediately over a window which would have been a wooden closure when the building had been a warehouse. Now a triangled sign beside the huge doors announced it to be a motor vehicle testing station and workshop.

I was trying to peer between the meeting of the two doors when a voice with a marked degree of challenge said: 'Can I help you?'

I was so startled that I answered with the very first thought that came into my head: 'Mr Mills?'

Amazingly the use of the name Mills seemed to dispel some of the hostility and he answered: 'No. I have just taken the boss in to Bournemouth station to get the London train. He has had a family bereavement and didn't feel like driving all that way. My name's Johnson, anything I can do?'

With so much having fallen into my lap in the previous half minute, a mood of in for a penny, in for a pound came over me and I ventured: 'Well no, it's just that Colin Townsend asked me to call when passing.' A long deeply quizzical look and for just a fleeting moment I thought he was ready to open up a conversation concerning Townsend, Mills or both, but he just as swiftly retreated into a cautionary shell.

By now he had, with huge keys, opened up the two correspondingly large padlocks, one a third of the distance down from the top of the doors, the other an equal measurement up from the bottom. Padlocks off, hasps eased away and the two great doors swung inward to reveal a large, very neat and totally enclosed workshop. The centre of the floor was entirely clear with sufficient space for a vehicle of any standard size. There was no pit in the floor but at the right hand wall stood a four wheel hydraulic raising jack and over head an iron girder supporting a moveable hoist with its series of pullies and chains to haul up the engine of any vehicle.

Two inch batoning around all of the panels which made up the walls each about four feet or so from the next enhanced a look of neatness not usually associated with motor vehicle worshops. The wall opposite to the doors was lined with shelves eighteen inches or a little more apart and from that distance above floor level up to arm reaching height. Upon them containers of oil, grease, flushing solvents, anti-freeze and a host of car accessory products. Perhaps only a small percentage for use in the course of servicing, the rest, I thought, to be retailed to would be purchasers.

It was time to take a second look at Johnson and to engage him in conversation from which I might glean information about himself, Mr Mills and the premises.

He was approaching forty, not more than five feet eight

inches tall, round face and dark hair thinning back from the temples to the crown of his head. It was however, his use of his eyes that I found most noticeable: of hardly average intellect and certainly not quick witted he appeared at all times to be vigilantly defensive.

In an attempt to find out what lay to the rear of the workshop I asked if a yard were not desirable mentioning that I had seen many similar lock-up workshops in France and Spain. He replied that there were no problems. Only work capable of commencement that day was booked in. Vehicles waiting to be serviced plus those completed and awaiting collection were parked in Clifton Road.

'Have you been with Mr Mills long?'

'I was with him when he had the garage just into the edge of town. We did everything there. Then about three years ago he got a bit of money together and turned the garage into a self-service petrol forecourt with a fellow on the till and a girl in the shop. He wanted to rent this place from old Barraclough but Barraclough wouldn't agree to the necessary work being done, so Mr Mills got some more cash and bought this and the place in Charlton Road where our auto-electrics workshop is, from him.'

'Separate electronic servicing,' I said sounding most impressed. 'I have never seen that equipment. I understand the results are fantastic.'

I knew that it had worked as he said: 'I'll take you round if you would like to see it. It is a very quiet day, with Mr Mills problems we cancelled a lot of work. I have a couple of things to do here though.' I felt sure that to anyone whom he accepted he could be an affable chatty companion but that I would have to prove quite a lot before he would accept me. I was convinced that even now he was telling me only what he wished to say or that which he had been instructed to say.

I wandered over once again to the rear wall and its

shelving. I had been puzzled by it and I was beginning to realise why. The shelving to the right hand side and to the left hand side was made up of equal perfectly cut lengths each one butted on to the next immediately in front of the respective two inch batons. At the centre section of the wall, however, the shelves extended beyond the upright baton, some by only three to four inches, some by seven and a couple by as much as ten. Although there were items on some shelves immediately in front of the batoning the line of shelf ends meeting was not one above the other and out of keeping with the symmetry of the work as a whole. As my mind searched for a reason my hand stretched out to remove a tin of high grade engine oil from the shelf in front of me but it was well and securely stuck to the shelf. I tried three tins of wax polish arranged together and the result was the same with all three.

Johnson had been watching and came over saying: 'They are for show, there. We take from the corner here to sell,' pointing to his right. 'Come and have a cup of tea in the cubby-hole,' and he almost led me away to an eight feet by eight feet room built on to the main road wall, between the entrance doors and the one toilet which was in the corner. His cubby-hole consisted of a sink with draining board and continuing bench upon which was a gas ring alight under a kettle already steaming. A wooden table, two chairs and a cupboard plus a wall telephone made up the furnishing, but like the rest of the workshop it was neat and clean.

Sitting there and enjoying a refreshing cup of tea I praised the conversion from warehouse to workshop and in one more attempt to obtain information asked if it had been carried out by a local firm. His answer did not surprise me: 'Good Lord no. You can't get the sort of work down here that Mr Mills wanted done. He might have gone to Bournemouth I suppose but he knew just the people he wanted, in London. And now if you still want to see it I'll show you the other workshop. Before hanging a card sign on a hook at the entrance he went to great lengths to draw my attention to it. It read, 'Back in five minutes'. I got the message.

We walked the fifty or so yards of the main road, continued for a similar distance into Clifton Road, first right and again first right brought us into Charlton Road. As we walked, he stressed his contention that two inter connected trades if not under one roof, should be side by side 'But down here that would have meant purpose built premises.'

From the corner of Clifton Road to the corner of Charlton Road I had silently counted my paces as we walked. It was one hundred and two. Allowing for the fact that we were walking and not striding out, I estimated the distance to be sixty-five yards. When moving about the first workshop I had estimated a front to rear distance of fifty to fifty-five feet. I was reasonably certain that the measurements in the premises we were approaching would be somewhat similar. A simple calculation and I realised that between the rear walls of each of the workshops was a distance of about eighty feet about which I still knew nothing. A situation I would be unlikely to alter while in the company of Johnson.

As he unlocked the doors Johnson said that were it not for the absence of Mills and that of a young trainee, both depots would have been open. Inside, except for the omission of heavy equipment and the cubby-hole rest room we might well have been standing in the first workshop. I merely glanced at the shelving to the far wall. Once again the semblance was almost identical except of course for the articles placed upon them. Here were batteries, volt meters, lamps and lights, jump leads and battery chargers. I was anxious not to alert Johnson to my new felt interest so did not test that of which I was certain: that the items at the centre were secured to the shelves.

On leaving him I expressed my thanks, as with fingers crossed I put it, from one who had lived a few of his early years in the area. It had been a game of give nothing away and I was prepared to concede that he had not lost.

As I made my way to the car a light aircraft flew overhead. With the car door unlocked and open, my body half in and half out of the driving seat, I became aware that I was talking to myself, or thinking aloud as I prefer to put it. 'The aircraft, the strip! Airstrip, airfield! Boulting's cabin is on the airfield, and somewhere closeby that's for sure.'

I re-secured the car and with bounding steps of renewed enthusiasm made my way to the little pub, The Ship. Just one central door to the front leading to a short narrow passage, door left — public bar, door right — saloon. I looked into the public bar, two young fellows were playing darts. I looked at them again, quickly. Mohican hair cuts. Down here! I thought that we had all of them corralled in the London area. The saloon was much more promising. Three men of similar age sitting together, retirees I guessed. An abundance of local knowledge waiting for a naive questioner such as myself. I had asked for my pint of beer at the bar but after my experience of the landlord of the Crown at Balham I decided to make my questions to the three wise men at the table.

My opening shot was: 'I am trying to contact Mr Boulting but so far I have failed to find the airstrip, is it far off?'

As if on command, three jugs were raised to three mouths, drained and returned firmly to the table top. I smiled and said to the landlord: 'Three more of whatever the gentlemen are having and one for yourself.'

The man nearest to where I was standing hooked the

leg of a chair with his feet and in the same motion pulled the chair up to the table, nodded his head from me to the chair and said: 'That's mighty nice of you, Sir. The field is not far. After Corfe take the fork to the right, then after a couple of miles take a right onto the B road marked to Lulworth, that will take you right to it. Gary Boulting will be up there now and until about dusk. He has a cottage on that road but prefers people to contact him at the cabin on the strip. Keeps 'isself to 'isself if you get me. Wanting flying lessons, is it?'

'Well yes, ultimately but I was hoping that he would take me for a flip around the area today and if I shape up, book me in for some lessons.'

'He'll take you if there is a chance. Ten quid is still ten quid in these parts.'

'Quite a character is Gary, do you know him at all Sir?' said one of the other two and realising my difficulty continued, 'I'm Fred,' and indicating the one who had been speaking, 'He's Ron,' and with a slide flick of his head to the third man, 'And he's Bob.'

'Thanks. No, Fred, I have never met him. His name was mentioned a while ago and I thought I would look him up and take it from there.'

'He's a Yank you know,' and Fred seemed pleased to have the story to tell. 'He and his identical twin brother came over with Cobden's Flying Circus. Alike as two peas they were and just about the stars of the show. You would have had as much of a job to tell them apart on the ground as you would their identical planes in the air.'

The beer jugs were looking a little on the low side and I motioned to the landlord to top up, at which all three were raised with alacrity. Fred continued: 'The shows were held on open fields near to coast holiday resorts. Gary and his brother James were absolute daredevils. The high spot was when they flew directly head on at one another not much above the ground and only at the last possible moment did Gary lift his plane above that of his brother. It was a terric show, but due to our summers and crowd safety restrictions it was not a financial success. All except Gary and James went back to America. Those two took over the flying club and flying school but three, maybe four years ago James went, we believe to America, and we think that perhaps there was not enough in it for two of them to make a living.'

Saying that it was time I pushed on up to the field. I left but not before quietly asking the landlord to take for one more round to be served after I had gone. It had been a time when I had learned a lot about the man whom I was now going eagerly to meet and all because a tiny plane flew overhead.

I found the field without trouble and could readily recognise the flying club end from the number of assorted light aicraft standing there. A high wooden wall, some forty feet in length had been erected against the prevailing winds. Projected forward from the top and onto posts of the same height with connecting rails at the top was a roof of heavy plastic material. There were large heavy waterproof canvas sheets with tie-ropes making up a bad weather hanger for a number of light aicraft.

At the other end of the field I found the cabin. It was so named on a board over the door. There was a sparsely furnished room for, I would imagine, pupils, passengers and anyone else other than Gary Boulting. His den would be the door marked office. Another room, with the door ajar, I could see to be a locker room with flying gear and parachutes neatly placed on large, sectioned shelving. The remaining door which was closed, I thought perhaps concealed a store room and it was from there that a large well-built man of forty plus emerged, turned and locked the door.

He saw me and came over with hand outstretched and said: 'Do I know you?' From the mouth upward his large face was almost covered by a combination of sideburns and moustache. His eyes were bright, bluish but not steely, rather kindly if not warm.

'I rather think not. My name is Diamond. Your name was mentioned and at last I have found the opportunity to ask if you will consider giving me lessons starting in about one month from now. Also, if you could possibly take me today for a short local flight, over the area where I spent the early years of my childhood. I do not expect to recognise any of it. It would be more in the nature of a sentimental journey really.'

'Well now, first I would not consider giving you lessons or anything else.' I saw the smile on his face as he spoke with a not unpleasant American drawl.

'I sell lessons and they don't come cheap. I am into flying strictly for the cash. If you have it in you I'll make a damn good flyer of you. I offer value for money but it's the money that talks. As to this afternoon: yes you are on, but it will cost you twenty-five of your English pounds for me to lift the wheels off the ground, by that I mean one of my short flights of around eight minutes in the air. For your lessons my fee will be sixty per hour and I will have you to flying club standard in under ten hours. Beyond that, how far you go in flying will be entirely up to you.'

'That sounds great and I would like the trip now. In fact, if you are prepared to accept my cheque I would prefer to make it a double.'

'Right, but twenty-five cash and twenty-five cheque. Let's find you a helmet and overalls and I'll take you in the two seater, far superior for map reading and I can come down quite a bit without upsetting the natives.'

In the locker room, as he removed his jacket before donning overalls, a small strip of paper with a broken rather

92

than torn end fell to the floor. I picked it up and handed it to him without comment. It had printing and a stamp mark on it. It was part of a band the function of which is to hold together a bundle of bank notes.

Indicating with his hands everything around him, the words fell easily from his lips:

'In this sort of business, the moment after you have called in at the bank it has all disappeared.'

He had a sure and deft touch when flying an aircraft. The plane sped across the field and after lift-off gave the appearance of standing on a wing tip and in a trice we were heading in the opposite direction. It was a trainer and we had two-way communication through the mike and earphones fitted into the helmets.

'Where did you live as a lad?'

'Clifton Road but if it is at all troublesome I am more than content to be over the area.'

'Troublesome for Gary Boulting,' he scoffed. 'Just give me the street number and we will knock on the door.'

As I got used to looking at the ground I could pick out various features. A long perspex canopy covered us both. As it extended downwards to just below shoulder height we had an uninterrupted view all round. As we approached at right angles to the A351 road he banked the aicraft making a tight left hand turn. Levelling out we were soon over the built up area and across the gap to Clifton and the surrounding roads. I got a glimpse of the Mills properties but too fleeting to take anything in. A little beyond the far end of Clifton Road he made a tight turn to come back on a reciprocal heading and at the same time reduced the engine to idling and we glided, almost silently, down to not more than twice roof top height. As we crossed the end of Clifton Road I could clearly see the workshops. As we passed over I could see the space between them. It was a yard and in it I saw an oblong of green. Boulting opened the throttle and pulled up and away. I turned my head and got a perfect view of a green van standing between those two workshops. His voice sounded again in my ears:

'Anything more you wish to see down there.'

'No, thank you so much, it was just wonderful. Is there time to get a look at the coast before the taxi-meter runs out.'

I had seen what I came to find and now looked forward to some minutes of superlative flying which I felt sure he had determined to show me. But no, he climbed to about three thousand feet and flew straight and level towards Swanage. His voice came again and it was as though a chill wind held me as he said:

'Roger Diamond. You realise that I could have killed you back there and still could now if it became a necessity. I have an ejector seat and you have not. As I told you earlier the only motivation I experience is the transfer of money, just one way — to me. I haven't the time or inclination to take sides in anything. I sell flying but at a price — my price. I have a terrifically lucrative contract going now. It is about the tenth such, although I have a feeling that it may be the last. Everyone is getting more than a little edgy. The operators are looking over their shoulders, looking after number one and that ain't good for me, one of their hired hands with no stake in the project. I have earned a tidy sum and when the fawcet begins to run dry I shall be heading stateside as fast as determination and dollars can get me there. I am sure that you are not police or you would have had back-up when you came down here and I feel sure that you have no more wish to threaten me than I you, but I will not look kindly on any move that brings to an early end the sweet little earner I am engaged in at present.'

There was a pause and I flicked the mike on and confirmed his supposition that I was not police.

94

'Two of my friends were so reduced in morale by these people that they came close to taking their own lives and one is not out of danger from them yet. To put an end to that is my motivation. Beyond that, like you, I have no quarrel with anyone not directly involved.'

As I finished he came back with: 'I knew that I had sized you up aright, I very rarely fail. In the same way I can usually sense the cruel bastards of this world and you my friend, are up against some of the meanest. I know that you know they know all about you, if you get my meaning. I cannot say that I know anyone at the top table but if those I have dealt with are anything to go by — watch out. If their precious scheme, whatever it is, goes wrong your life will not be worth a plugged nickel as any old westerner would say. They gave me timely warning of a possible visit and looking at you I have to admit that the description of you was absolutely spot on. Now you may not have noticed but we are heading back and close to the field. When we land I want you to change and take your leave of me in the most natural way you know how. If you are in the States later look me up. I'll probably be grubbing around a flying field but for now just drive. Their success is that everyone is watched and that especially includes me. So long Mr Diamond.' A chuckle came into his voice as he finished with: 'Oh by the way I haven't an ejector seat either.' He made his way to the cabin alone, purposefully, I thought, and I divested myself of helmet and overalls while still beside the plane.

12

I drove from the field and after a short while joined the traffic on the A351 and at about four-thirty pulled in once again to the car park of the Tree Tops hotel. Booking in at reception I was offered and accepted the same room. The service, as ever, flawless and friendly, no raised eyebrows to find me still alone but a trace of genuine pleasure when I said I would like to put through a call to Mrs Garland immediately on going to the room. I did just that and it was Helen who answered when the call reached her office.

I had not expected that it would be easy for either of us in this our first conversation since the astounding events here in this room some eighteen hours earlier. My opening approach: 'How are you Pet?' met with the cool, composed, I'm in command Helenism I had known from day one; until the previous night, that is.

'Where have you been Roger? I rang the hotel and they told me you had left. Where are you now?'

'Here at Tree Tops.'

'Oh you are back there, why did you not follow me back here?'

'From the manner in which you left I was sure that you, that perhaps we both needed some time of soothing reflection.'

'Soothing reflection! You chase around after a Colin Townsend who could be a million miles away and you call that soothing reflection?'

'I didn't say so but yes,' I came back sharply. 'I did not catch up with him but I did with Mills and Boulting,

96

on whom he had no doubt called.'

'Roger you will be killed, you will be killed,' she said with such an abundance of emotion.

My voice softened as I came out with the corny cliche: 'I didn't know you cared.'

'I don't, well, yes I do,' she answered and for the first time falteringly, 'You charge around seeking trouble. There is no need for you to be killed or even hurt if you will only stop now. Why not return at once and we can dine out and spend a lovely evening together? Lord Garland would welcome our return to normal working and being here together could provide another chance to get to know each other well.' The tone of voice left very little doubt of an intention to appeal to sensual instincts.

'Dearest Helen, you would do anything to remove me from danger. This evening though I have to find a dentist to do an emergency on this tooth of mine, the jip now and again was bearable but for the past hour it has been non stop. I know that I have an appointment booked with the Aussie dentist in the Strand but cannot for the life of me remember which day that is. In any event I must get some temporary relief this evening or go stark staring bonkers. I shall come back tomorrow but Pet, whatever old Garland says, with that which you and I have uncovered I must go to the police if we are to pull out now.'

The staccato almost ranting voice, reminiscent of our first meeting, snapped from the earpiece: 'Sign your own death warrant, I cannot save you now. Go to hell, go to hell!' A click and the line was dead. I was startled but thought only of having read or having been told that women can behave quite violently to loved ones whom they perceive to be in danger.

So she loved me.

The ever dependable reception desk found a dentist for me but I would have to sit it out in the waiting room in the hope of a break between appointments. Address 251, Christchurch Road, Mr Golightly. What an absolute peach of a name for a dentist — Golightly. The one thing I could not have done then was drive my car, a fact mentioned to the receptionist and as I walked across the main hall a taxi pulled up at the entrance.

As I entered the surgery two ladies were seated in the waiting room. The apprehensive look on both faces convinced me that it was not an occasion on which I could ask to queue jump.

Moving along past the low coffee type table I scanned the magazines on parade. Nothing on cars, a couple on gardening but both with more words than pictures or diagrams. Reading held no appeal whatsoever, but pictures I could stand while waiting until Mr Golightly would make the pain go away. In one corner there was a small table and upon it a stack of assorted magazines. I rummaged through the top few and pulled out a copy of *Who Ever* which I recalled to be an up-market picture magazine which I thought had failed about six months after its launch, a few years back. The simple answer was revealed when I noticed that this copy was almost four years old but pictures there would be and I made my way back to my chair thinking that Dentists had probably got the edge over Doctors in the matter of preserving golden oldies. I have no particular interest in how the other half live so it became just a browse through. That was until my frenzied turn back of the page I had started to turn on, to confirm that I had caught sight of a photograph of Helen. There she was younger but as regal in appearance as now. At her right wrist hung a very attractive band of link weave gold bracelet, an exquisite example of the craftsman's art. I had seen it before, beneath the light of the desk lamp in Fergie's room. Beside her a fellow with the awful combination of a podgy face and a weak chin. I am sorry but I will never be able to separate and enumerate the many emotions and afflictions that seized me in those few seconds. I was dazed as I read from below the photograph: 'Helena Mandorff with Bertram Garland, son of newly created life peer and Lord Chancellor designate Lord Garland, in a specially posed photograph on the occasion of their engagement. They plan to marry in the early autumn.'

I closed the magazine but could not release it from my hand. Suddenly my world was an unsure place. I made to stand but my knees were unsure that they could support my weight and I slumped back upon the chair. The dental receptionist had noticed my distress and on her offer of help I reminded her that I had come with a rather nasty toothache but that I was now feeling a little unwell. She went into the surgery, I assumed to talk with Mr Golightly and within five minutes after her return I was shown into the surgery and seated in the dental chair.

Small X-rays were taken of the offending side of my jaw and having examined them Mr Golightly informed me that the problem was a small abcess to the gum at the rear of one of my teeth. He could not be absolutely sure but held a certain amount of confidence that the tooth would prove to be clean, as he put it. He proposed to give me injections and the pain would commence to abate later that evening. The abcess would self discharge, probably the next day. His dental assistant would give me some medicated mouth wash for use at that time. He quite understood that, as I lived in London, I would be going to my own dentist and he could supply me with a note explaining his diagnosis and treatment for me to pass on to my own dentist. His fee would be eighteen pounds and fifty pence.

I remain very grateful to Mr Golightly. His logical recital of his own actions and proposals obliged me to put my confused and troubled thoughts in order and construct and review proposals that might extricate me from what was potentially a far more dangerous situation than I had hitherto imagined.

On the basis of what was now clear in my mind, despite the upset experienced in having to suddenly reappraise a remarkable personal relationship, Lord Garland was undoubtedly number one in whatever the true purposes of the New Citizens League ultimately revealed itself to be. Was Helen then, second in command or just a helper because of family ties. Was husband Bertram number two in which case the pressure on Helen to take part would have been even more compelling.

As I thought back I recalled the cat and mouse game in which I had engaged Johnson at the Mills workshop with each of us quite sure of the real identity of the other. Of the friendly but none-the-less formidable warning given to me by Gary Boulting and now the impact of this new and devastating revelation caused me to realise that, as I progressed toward unravelling the puzzle, so personal danger had been closing in on me. Helen had been in the perfect position to monitor the developing threat that I had become and to report to Lord Garland when that threat had to be eliminated. The words 'sign your own death warrant I cannot save you now' that Helen had used over the telephone such a short while before, indicated that the time had arrived.

I determined that I would not now return to the hotel or indeed to my car. Instead I travelled by taxi to Bournemouth Central railway station and after checking the train times, went to a public pay phone where I dialled the contact number to Superintendent Johnny Cousens. It was not Johnny but the voice on the ansaphone. Remembering not to give my name or any form of identification, at the tone I said:

'Events are almost at crisis point. I am catching the seven-twelve. I am sorry but I appear to be in some danger.'

I had intentionally omitted any reference to Bournemouth for the obvious reason. It had been the last place from which I had made contact and he would only expect me to refer to a new location.

On the train I found it almost impossible to read either the evening newspaper or the magazine that I had purchased just before boarding, or look again at that old copy of *Who Ever* which haunted me so and which I still retained. It is a strange but true fact that when one is in a similar position to that in which I found myself, the bland and innocuous stare from someone opposite takes on a new and almost sinister meaning.

Not a relaxed and easy journey but Waterloo station and the hustle bustle of people appeared, as it should, to be perfectly normal. As I approached the ticket barrier I saw Johnny just beyond. He recognised me and made a small signalling motion as he adjusted his hat. Preparing to give up my ticket something within my head whispered 'Thank God for the Johnny Cousens of this world'. He stepped forward to greet me, warmly and reassuringly. We said little, mainly inadequacies such as 'Good to see you' and 'Did you have a good trip?', as he motioned me to a car already drawn up on the narrow road that divides the concourse. As we did so one of his men who had been unobtrusively ambling in the area, ever vigilantly, moved closer to us until we were beside it.

Two men were already seated in the front as we took our place in the rear of the car. Johnny introduced them as Chief Inspector George Dodds and at the wheel Sergeant Roy Davis, adding that George had been keeping a watchful eye on Tony Fairchild but that so far they had been enjoying an uneventful existence.

'And it is to Tony we are heading now.'

I looked out, surprised that we were already turning from

Kennington Road into the narrow entrance that leads to Arbinger Square. Tony and Carol were so delighted to see me one would have thought that it had been months instead of days. Johnny Cousens had called there earlier, before going on to Waterloo and, as a result, I was to stay the night. My future movements were to be decided after they had heard the full story and Johnny had assessed the probabilities.

Carol had sensibly prepared snacks that could be finger eaten as we talked. She lingered as she approached the door. Johnny looked at me and I nodded. He put out a hand to touch her arm as she passed and said: 'Do stay Mrs Fairchild, we are not about to discuss state secrets.' Sergeant Davis sought permission and left to go to the local nick as he preferred to call it, to play a game of snooker. He would be just a phone call away when required to collect the two senior officers.

Except for Carol, of course, they had been kept up to date by Johnny, up to date that is, to the point of our conversation of the previous evening. I then recounted the events in which I had been involved from that moment on briefly but trying to ensure that all I considered to be salient points were not overlooked. I took them chronologically: the argument at dinner, the fiasco in the bedroom, Mill's workshops and Johnson, the colourful Gary Boulting, the disastrous attempt at a would be reconciling telephone call to Helen and I finished by showing them the photograph in *Who Ever* which needed no words from me to emphasise the dramatic turnabout it signalled for each and everyone of us.

They all listened very intently, Carol providing the feminine touch by at times, looking quite aghast. But it was Johnny who spoke:

'Roger, I do now regret having given you qualified assurances earlier that the risks were minimal but both you and they have moved up a couple of gears in the past forty-eight hours. I would like us to review the various incidents since you were projected into the arena by Mr Ferguson, in the light of what we have just learned. However, I would mention in passing that your, how can I put it kindly, charisma did strike a chord in Helen Mandrake and that may well have saved you from rough treatment. According to the influence she has within this league, she may well continue to do so, provided we ensure that you cease playing an investigative role in respect of their activities. You will see that unless we can restore you to your working environment together with a display of conforming to Helen's entreaty they will continue to be increasingly nervous and suspicious concerning you. And we would find it difficult to afford one hundred per cent safety other than by exporting you until this sordid charade is over. The police have no intention of underestimating its importance but want to keep it in perspective. 'George, have you anything you wish to add before we take a fresh look at past events?'

'Just to assure Roger and Tony that in anything they may volunteer to do they will have the same and, if possible, more back-up than if they were our own men.' Johnny Cousens looked towards and asked 'Tony?'

'Well yes, glad to have you here Roger. Tomorrow you will look back with pride and I with envy, at all that you have achieved,' and lowering his hand upon Carol's, 'Mark you, there are some parts that we happily married men would have found difficult to play.' Which brought a chuckle from us all, not least from Carol.

And so we moved to the inquest on the past, as someone put it. Johnny proposed that in each case he would outline the obvious and we comment or if necessary discuss the implications.

'At Ferguson's room Helen realised the switch and

103

informed Townsend, but they decided to act as though they believed it to be him. She might not have known that it was Roger but she was very capable of finding out. The security men at the main entrance, in answer to a question, would have told her that it was you making enquiries about the visitors to Mr Ferguson.'

'But I told her that it was me at the little personnel room.'

'That is so but she already knew. You were early that morning and went directly to that room. It must have been more than coincidence that Helen, too, was early and went to that room which would hardly qualify for overall supervision at that hour.'

Tony said: 'Why did they not leave when they recognised the switch and so obviate the risk of exposure.'

And Chief Inspector Dodds replied: 'They had no idea of Ferguson's whereabouts and wanted him to believe that his ploy had succeeded.'

I asked: 'With the new knowledge of Helen's probable importance to the league and Townsend's recent role, was this not an over the top team to threaten Fergie.'

'We will only know the answer to that when we learn the importance of Ferguson to them.' This from Johnny who continued: 'At Mastersons and the pub opposite. I think that the only point here is that if and when Masterson or his goons telephoned descriptions of Roger and Tony, Helen was the person who could give those descriptions identities and assure Masterson that you were not police officers.' The rest of us indicated agreement.

'The journey to Guildford or rather Guildford railway station, a big disappointment for Roger who had read the clues well and handled the observation skilfully but as we now know, with both hands tied behind his back, so to speak. In the light of present knowledge Helen was in command right from the start. She would have given Townsend early warning and train times that made the

Guildford switch a certainty. Further consultation, or maybe just instruction, as she stood beside him at Waterloo station and then at only the expense of being thought a fool commits the gaffe that ensured his complete getaway.'

From George Dodds: 'The possible roles of Lord Garland and Helen Mandrake respectively or collectively are yet to be revealed but if she is just his family helper I would fear mental combat with his right hand man.' From the rest of us, no comment. Johnny then made what he said was a general observation.

'I think that you were watched from the time of the Ferguson room incident but they lost you when you set off for Mastersons from Tony's address but picked you up again when you left early for the visit to the personnel office. The tail was, of course, done away with once Helen, with Lord Garland's connivance and your ready agreement, took over your close supervision herself. How priceless for Lord Garland to say that he did not wish to be troubled with reports and requests for permission. That you two should agree decisions. Helen Mandrake's decisions and Helen Mandrake reported to him as many times a day as was necessary.'

With a sheepish grin I said: 'Do you wish the withdrawal of the application to join your team that I was considering making, as of now?'

'Roger my friend, without the information which you have just now given, most and perhaps all of us would have acted in exactly the same way. The big chief of a large and important government department asks if you can discreetly help to find just what is causing a smell and without calling us in. No, I would be proud to have you as one of my team.' Turning to me he said: 'Roger, would you like to tell us how you view events of the past thirty-six or so hours, both then and now? I ask for two reasons. We would get your first hand recollection and reaction and you may welcome the benefit of talking therapy in respect of something you would really wish to erase from thought.'

'Thank you yes. The only handicap I felt at the time was the restriction you had placed on me, Johnny, curbing my conversations with Helen to the extent that I could not make a good personal case in our choice of where to stay or what to do. You had told me of the security van stop over at Southampton. I suggested to Helen that we make a stop there. She made a very good case for Bournemouth with its amenities and excellent choice of hotels. Had I been able to mention the van and consequent probability that Townsend would be in the area it would have been reasonable to expect that she would have been keen to be there with me, in our quest for Townsend. I realise now, that she too would have known of the van and of its arrival in Southampton. Then on my request to go there and mentioning the van, she would still have done anything to prevent our going there. After my next call when you mentioned losing the van in the Corfe Castle area, I strongly proposed that we go down ourselves in that direction but under the Superintendent gag I was forced to add very lamely, to find Townsend. Later when I again urged that we go along the A351 road in search of him she er' she er.'

'She made you an offer you could not refuse,' Carol said sympathetically. 'Something like that,' I answered gratefully. 'And now of course, I realise that I held no irresistable charm, quite the contrary and that what she did then is a measure of how much support she is prepared to give to her husband and to Lord Garland in whatever it is they are trying to achieve. Of the van in the workshop I would only add my hope that your men now have it and it affords the forensic evidence I read so much about. With regard to Gary Boulting you will realise that I have reason to be very, very grateful to him. Even without that debt

I would sum up my assessment of Mr Boulting as bent but not crooked.

I would like to tell you that I have the most bizarre hunch concerning what I will call the end of the line. If I am right it could make a big contribution to bringing an end to this nightmare, but if wrong I would like to confine my chagrin to myelf with condolences only from Tony and Carol. Superintendent, I do feel that I should be formal in making a request. I am of course, aware that there is a point at which you would feel obliged to detain someone you knew to have commited a more than trivial offence. This has I assure you nothing to do with my gratitude to Boulting but I cannot put my hunch to the test unless he is at large. If Tony and I, with agreement and a little help from Carol, go on a trip commencing on Friday my hunch will have been proved or otherwise before the weekend.

He answered very graciously: 'I accept and respect your wishes in the matter of your hunch as you put it. I recall experiments that I made privately and only to be divulged if the result was a success. Tony and Carol will speak for themselves but I will be delighted if you are teamed up together. I am sure you are first class at taking care of one another. Now Boulting, may I put it this way, unless he does something to force my hand and bearing in mind that he is operating in another police area, I gladly agree and of course believe your reasons.'

Tony said: 'Why Friday, why not tomorrow?' And Carol predictably said: 'What grubby little job do I get while you two get all of the fun.'

'Tomorrow I am going to make friendly and peaceful surrender to the wishes of Helen. I shall tell her that I propose spending three days with you two in your native Leicestershire in an attempt to get the whole wretched business out of my mind or out of my hair, whichever one is troubling me the most. And if you agree Carol, I would like you to be the decoy, the only one who ultimately gets there, while Tony, if he agrees, and I take a vastly different route.'

Johnny Cousens said that he was glad to hear that a decoy was to be used: 'Do take care,' he added. 'You will be watched, particularly you Roger, now that Helen can no longer shadow you herself. Chief Inspector Dodds and I are bound by the Official Secrets Act, so suffice it to say that MI5, MI6 and Special Branch, that's us, are aware of many things apropos the League. We have it under watchful review, particularly since your experience brought to light their methods of coercion.' Turning to Carol he said: 'And now if I may use your telephone I will bring to an end the winning or losing streak of young Roy Davis at the snooker table.'

13

It was no more than seven-thirty in the morning when Johnny telephoned me at Kennington to say that my car with my overnight bag in it was being driven up from Bournemouth and would arrive before noon. I could not remember him asking for the keys. He also told me of a visit to the Tree Tops hotel at one o'clock in the morning by two men asking for me. They would not give names or state their business. On being told that I was not in my room they demanded the key to check for themselves and became verbally abusive to the night porter when he refused. They left hurredly when he used the telephone to call the police. With the seriousness of his message sounding in his voice he continued: 'Do keep in mind Roger that this was only eight hours after Helen Mandrake had learned that you were back at the hotel.'

Mental rehearsals in which I had engaged earlier of just how to approach Helen with my new acceptance of if you can't beat 'em, pack it in, proved unnecessary when at three minutes after half past nine she came into my room. The one difference from previous such moments was in my perception of her. Her physical presence which I had thought of in awe and spoken of as regal I now viewed as haughty, and words that I would have clung to as demonstrating interest in me I now heard as incisive interrogation. But to my disquiet I was aware that I continued to be fascinated by her.

'I rang the hotel again and was informed that you had left.' That could not be true but I simply answered: 'I had left to go to the dentist.'

'But you did leave. Did you come up by train?'

'Yes, by the seven-twelve.'

'Then why the heck did you not contact me? We could have had a lovely evening together.'

'I was tired, you were upset and I just had to contact my friends about our weekend which had been arranged but not finalised.'

'Did you go back to your place? I rang a couple of times.'

'No, as I said I was tired, more so after a meal and they put me up for the night.'

'Where is their place?'

'Kennington.' And being unable to resist one tiny dig of defiance: 'I am sure that you know it.'

I had fenced well, causing her to take the initiative when she said: 'Roger it is because I am concerned for your safety, as I am for my own, that I said what I did. How do you feel about the whole thing now?'

'Oh, I agree with you, I did last evening I suppose. I just needed a little time to think.'

'And do you not agree there is nothing you and I can do to assist Mr Ferguson and Mr Cartwright further?'

'Yes, you are right Helen, I have no wish to become more involved. I think that I am more cut out for the easy quiet life.'

So there it was, complete capitulation as prescribed by Johnny Cousens. She accepted it calmly and without visible pleasure. In fact, exactly as I would have expected of Helen Mandrake I thought I knew previously. She appeared satisfied that further persuasion was unnecessary and she did not suggest or even hint at a lunch date, an evening meal or future assignation. For my part I was relieved. However, at one-fifteen on returning to my room I found Helen waiting for me.

With a quisical look she said: 'You travelled up on the train but your car is here in the car park.' I speedily recalled that when asking me to contact security at the gates to facilitate admission for the driver of my car, Johnny Cousens had said that at all checks and barriers the driver would make a point of saying that he had been engaged by the management of the Tree Tops hotel to drive the car to London. And so it was with calm composure of certitude I replied to Helen: 'They promised to deliver it to me here. I hate to think what the bill will be.'

Having looked forward to a quiet evening with Tony and Carol running through the weekend itinerary, I was surprised and not overpleased to get a call from Johnny. The only identification was his voice as with the utmost economy with words he said, 'I thought we might have a drink. Seven-thirty alright with you?' And as soon as I managed: 'Yes fine,' he closed with: 'See you then, bye.'

He had previously informed me that, although he had no intention of using my place of work as a point of contact, he would do so if it became really necessary, and so the reason for our meeting was something that could not wait until after the weekend. I would now go first to my hotel to change and pack a bag, from there to our rendezvous pub, and only after that on to Carol and Tony. I managed to get Tony on the internal to say, with regret, that it would be eight-thirty before I could arrive at their place.

At the agreed seven-thirty I arrived at the top end of Carnaby Street with packed bag and dressed with the intention of resembling a holiday making tourist. I met Johnny coming from the opposite direction and we turned together into the bar. For him the pin-striped suit had given way to slacks and slicker. With a grin I said:

'But you are not invited,' which brought the equally smiling riposte:

'I very rarely am.'

Two swigs of beer allowed sufficient time to glance around the bar and its customers before he said: 'Sorry to bring you out at short notice but I have only now received a third item of information which together with the other two makes for great interest. Grainger, in the talks we had with him, twice mentioned La Salle et Cie. of Rouen. Then our enquiries which, as I have already mentioned are going on independently of your own, came up with a reference to La Salle et Cie., Bankers, of Rue de Charenton, Rouen. And, just this morning, I received a reply to my enquiry through Interpol, stating that in the matter of La Sale et Cie. there had been a take-over or merger four years ago in which an English syndicate was prominant.' He paused, for effect I felt sure, and continued: 'Now get this little gem Roger, among the English directors we find Bertram Garland and Colin Townsend.' All I could say was 'Good God!' He continued: 'So if during your trip you would do your friend a favour by turning the steering wheel in that direction and as naive Brits obtain some information as to how monies are paid in and paid out, I will be ever grateful.'

He merely raised his eyebrows to what on my face must have been a look of startled astonishment as I said: 'Is there anything that you do not know?'

Again the modesty 'Almost everything, it is you and those like you who produce the pegs, I just fit them into the right holes. Oh, one more news item, Grainger is back at his job after his period of sickness with us. He is so frightened of them and even more frightened of us, that he will not utter an ill considered word for a very long time to come.'

I looked at my watch. I had not wanted to come but was very pleased that I had. As we finished our drinks and prepared to leave he grinned: 'Have a good mystery trip. Everything you learn will be new and vital information for me.'

Arriving at Kennington with my watch showing eight

112

thirty-eight I made further apologies, this time to Carol directly. We enjoyed a delicious meal and after a combined washing up exercise settled down to discuss the proposed journeys of the next day. We were agreed on everything, accepting that we would be followed and that we must shake off our pursuers before reaching the start of the M.1. motorway, having been impressed by the way the security van had eluded police cars by creating a little distance just before a vital change of direction. Carol would drive and have the internal mirror and offside wing mirror retained in normal driving positions. Tony in the front passenger seat using the nearside wing mirror adjusted to an even more straight setting and the large cosmetic mirror on the underside of the sun visor, in an attempt to detect a vehicle content to be tucked in on the nearside with just a couple of cars between us and them. I took from my bag my large shaving mirror on a stand which, when swivelled, offered on one side magnification and on the other normal mirror. I told them I proposed sitting in the nearside corner of the rear seating holding the mirror in my right hand and by adjusting its position pick out quite a bit of vehicle movement behind us. But, although it was to be an early morning start, sunshine might make use of my mirror and that of the cosmetic one inadvisable. We realised that right or left hand turns would be detected as they were being made, however quickly. So, having first identified our pursuers we would await and indeed try to create, a situation where we could make a sufficiently late crossing on the change of lights causing our followers to be caught on red. Bearing in mind the change over cycle of lights Carol would drive on only sufficiently for Tony and I to bundle out and take what cover we could before the other vehicle reached that spot.

Carol would then commence her decoy act, making for the M.1. and increasing speed with the intention of remaining in front for as long as posisble, while Tony and I hopefully would get to a convenient underground station by taxi. From there to Waterloo and then by rail to Portsmouth, where Tony would hire a car and with it board the ferry for Cherbourg while I would join the same ferry as a foot passenger. We would link up together again once on French soil.

We all decided that to be enough planning to give us a more reasonable start to our proposed venture, and went to bed.

14

For the first few miles of driving out through north London, seemingly every other car was mentioned as a possible but as most of the other cars used opportunities to overtake and others made turnings off from our route we strived for patience, looking for one that had lived with us over a distance. As I recognised one matching that requirement Tony said:

'The mid-grey Citroen, two back on the nearside,' which was the very car I had in mind.

'I agree,' I confirmed, 'but its tinted glass makes it impossible to see who is in it.'

And Carol said: 'Which highlights difficulty for me once you two have baled out.'

'You will be just fine, Honey,' said Tony reassuringly. 'Once you have led them onto the motorway they will not be able to turn back to look for us until after quite a distance.'

The Citroen stayed with us but varied its relative position in the overall traffic. I asked Carol to gently reduce our speed by five or six miles per hour, which did present them with a difficulty. Cars no longer stayed between us, choosing instead to overtake and other vehicles that might have moved into the space carried on by passing both the Citroen and ourselves in one movement of overtaking. The driver of the Citroen was obliged to slow down even more in order to once again put one or two vehicles between us, rather than invite attention by sitting right on our tail.

'That is it, don't you agree Tony?' I murmured as though the situation called for whispering. 'If Carol can manouevre them into that sort of speed and position as we approach the lights, the model they are driving has relatively poor initial acceleration and Carol will have a chance to leave them stranded.'

'Yes that's just fine; Carol and I know this road well from our journeyings up to home.' And turning to his wife he said, 'Remember the three sets of lights, all within about a mile, they will be coming up shortly. Unless there is a clear cut opportunity I would, if I were you, do whatever comes naturally on the first one or even two, it will convince them that you are the lady driver who actually compiled the highway code. I will be your rally co-driver and whichever set of lights it is darling, when I give you Go, Go, Go, — foot smoothly but firmly down to the floor boards!'

The first two sets of lights came and went very much as Tony had predicted. After the second set I saw him tense as he took special note of everything around us. As the lights well ahead turned to green he seemingly began to count.

'Hold it at that,' he said to Carol, followed by 'Move up on the inside,' as a car immediately in front began to move out to the centre and at about one hundred or so yards from the crossing: 'Begin to step up darling, it will be seconds before they realise.' As the lights changed to amber and quite a bit short of the crossing his crisp voice rang out 'Go. Go. Go.' Carol did everything right, the car that had been in front and now beside us slowed and came to a stop but by that time we were over the junction. Looking back from the rear window I had seen the Citroen swing to the nearside in an attempt to follow the route we had taken but traffic from the left now having the green crossed its bows and although they passed the post bearing the lights they could not proceed one yard further, being prevented by solid cross traffic. There was no time for reaction of either elation or concern. The job was, as yet, only partly done. Then Carol saw the opportunity. There was a shopping precinct to which we were approaching on our nearside, with only a service road between us and it. Why I do not know but I pushed my shaving mirror under the front passenger seat and then took a firm hold of both my travel bag and Tony's. As the car pulled to a halt at the kerb, he and I swiftly left by the nearside doors, ran across the service road and through the partially open door of a shop directly in front of us only to find that it was exclusively for the sale of ladies lingerie. I stood amazed as Tony described two imaginary wives and at the conclusion asked if the said wives had already been into the shop. The charming lady behind the counter was so amused and bemused by our supposed predicament, she readily agreed to telephone for a taxi which arrived shortly and conveyed us to what turned out to be Arnos Grove underground station. From there to Waterloo and on to Portsmouth proved swift and uneventful and we were in that city a little before noon. The hiring of the car and boarding went very much according to our plan but by the time the ferry was a short distance out we had both decided our behaviour to be melodramatic.

We left the ferry together in the car and drove the dozen or so miles to Maupertus before turning north to the airport situated beside the road that leads up to Cap Levy.

The administrative offices were housed in a block of single storey buildings well to the right of, and remote from, the main passenger terminal and attendant buildings associated with the business of a small efficient airport. It was to the main entrance we were directed to complete some very sensible security vetting before proceeding along a service road, within the perimeter fence, to the local section where offices and general administration rooms for every type of light aircraft flying were to be found. Air taxi and hire services to flying club and flying school. Some light aircraft and helicopters stood on the tarmac apron in front of the buildings. Those buildings and a short runway for the use of small aircraft, presented no hazard or hindrance to the main section of the airport. As we came closer we were more aware of the movement of people, ground crew, flying personnel and office staff going about normal activity on a quite normal day. There was however nothing normal in the feeling of minor panic instilled within me at the sight of two fliers walking from the direction of the parked aircraft en route for the flight crew room, and the realisation that without a marked deviation they and we must pass very close to one another. They were well laden, each carrying two parachutes and a flying helmet. With so much safety equipment there was no mistaking them. Flying instructor and pupil.

The ten or more seconds taken to size them up and be sure served also to allow rational thought to take over. Quietly but clearly I said to Tony: 'The one on the right is Boulting, keep a conversation going and as they are doing the same I may pass unnoticed.' By then there was only a matter of feet between us and contrary to my hopes Boulting and I engaged in what is increasingly described as eyeball to eyeball confrontation. But there was not even a flicker of recognition.

'You were right about the sideburns and moustache,' said Tony, 'he certainly likes to draw attention to himself, but you got away with it alright.'

'I was right Tony, I was right,' the words spluttered from my lips. 'Not just now, but in my reasoning that brought us here. That Tony, is Boulting but not Gary Boulting. That is his identical twin, James.'

'But surely you were tipped off,' said a delightedly surprised Tony, 'It is too much of a coincidence that you pick this airfield in the hope of finding someone you have never seen.'

'Tipped off, well steered to by an item in the newspapers of about six months ago. It was sufficiently unusual to remain in my memory and on Thursday Chris Banks of the Press Association obtained for me a copy of the original article. A man, believed to be British, was stabbed to death in the course of being mugged just a short distance from the main entrance here. His attackers were disturbed and when challenged fled. In various compartments within his clothing, some originally pockets, plus specially stitched in envelopes, a fortune in large denomination English bank notes was found. The money was neither claimed nor traced to any person or persons and the poor man was not identified.'

'Tony, I think that as it is getting late, too late for trainer planes, in which we are now very interested, to be flying, we should call it a day. I would like us to come for a while tomorrow if you agree but before we leave and while I stay here to see just who comes and goes, would you take a look at the bunch of light aircraft from which Boulting emerged. One of the hunches you so often pull my leg about tells me that you may find a Proctor two seater trainer with British markings and stencilled on the side the registration G.D.1289. If I am right and there is an opportunity to glance at the tail plane, would you look for the letters R.D. of about half an inch by half an inch each on the left hand side of the tail fin and printed in biro.' He was gone for only three to four minutes. As he walked back to join me I could see pleased excitement on his face, in his walk and in his whole being. I signalled caution with a finger laid across my lips and fell in to walk with him in a manner suggesting having awaited his return from one of the offices or a visit to the toilet.

As we left the airport and returned to the car Tony said: 'I don't know how you do it, but one hundred per cent on the first part, the aircraft was there and exactly as you described it but there was no mark of lettering anywhere on the tail assembly.'

'That is every bit as I expected it to be. You will remember that late on Wednesday, at your home, I asked Superintendent Cousens for time and this trip to prove or disprove Gary Boulting's role and possible involvement in the whole damned business. Now that you have confirmed my suspicions and once you are fortified with an aperitif and a good meal I will be happy to outline my theory in the new knowledge that it must be right.'

We drove back to Cherbourg and intentionally avoided international and other large hotels, choosing instead the small and comfortable Coq d'Or. After a full and fairly exhausting day we visited the bar, the dining room and a quiet corner of the lounge in that order. Once seated in the corner we could not resist our recently acquired habit of having a good look around before speaking.

'The plane I described was identical to the one in which Gary Boulting flew with me over Corfe Castle and the coast. Identical but not the same. I can see from your face that you are with me. Two identical planes, even the registration has been made to coincide. And of course, two identical twin brothers, James in France, Gary in England. For James, observation of the details of his existance would be vital, airport taxes and charges, national taxes and reason for an American to be giving flying lessons in France, using an aircraft registered in Britain. We have seen the answer to the last one, today. To instruct pupils who have no command of the French language and are happier with instruction in clear English. As to the plane itself, well how about an assurance to the authorities that the next new one, due shortly, will be purchased and registered in France. So, now we have two identical set ups, the background to each being genuine flying instruction coupled with genuine pleasure flights. The number of illegal flights would have

120

been determined by the amount and availability of the stolen bank notes. At those particular times then, the two pilots together with two other men, part of the illicit transport clique, but posing as pupils, go to their aircraft at synchronised watch timing, in England and in France. Proof we will get but my guess is that the bank notes or whatever, are stowed in the four parachute casings carried to the plane. And from France, well it might just be the returned empties. Once again at a synchronised time something like a spin off the top of a loop brings each of the aircraft down to below radar scanning and think of the flying circus routine, Tony, but on these occasions without safety precaution or survival equipment, each procedes at wave top height, one to France the other to England. At precisely the correct point each climbs to, say, a couple of thousand feet, performs a few more exercises and lands at the others airfield. Parachutes to the crew room and later on to the car. Who is to question? Each at the home of the other and there to begin the process of laundering of which I hope we may find out more tomorrow.

On the Saturday morning we left the hotel for a second visit to the airfield, having agreed that the two most advantageous times for such an aerial manoeuvre would be during the early and late hours of daylight. Accepted once again through the security screening at the main entrance and having reached the local section, we entered the waiting room cum snack bar as the ideal place to avoid drawing attention to ourselves and having the other feature of importance to us, a large expanse of window looking out onto the apron and the runway beyond.

Thirty-seven minutes can, I suppose, seem interminable in very many situations. On that occasion, sufficiently long for doubt to threaten a feeling of success so far enjoyed. Of course, the chance that some form of activity, putting the correctness of my deduction beyond doubt, could not be more than a fifty-fifty one. We had been able to satisfy ourselves that the means to switch ill-gotten monies was present but the Superintendent would need more proof than we had in order to request the freezing of funds we had reason to believe might be held by La Salle et Cie. A niggling suspicion that I might have misread the scenario regarding the activities of Gary Boulting was a cause for disquiet, only to be partially set aside by the appearance of brother James, or was it perhaps Gary himself, coming from the crew room accompanied by a similarly, dressed for flying, man. A little older than I would have expected but in all other respects the archetypal pupil pilot. Both were wearing parachute harness and carrying helmet and extra chute. Tony said:

'I am prepared to make a small wager that each of the pupils on this particular exercise, were also members of Cobden's flying circus.'

'I will not throw away money by challenging that deduction however attractive you care to make the odds,' I laughed back at him. The flyers had reached the aircraft, the one Tony had examined the previous evening and quite shortly they were airborne and heading north in the direction of Cap Levy.

As we settled to the enforced period of waiting Tony said: 'You are rather loath to do anything that will set the gendarmes after the Boulting brothers aren't you?'

'I hadn't thought of it quite like that but the straight answer is yes, although it is not that simple. I would not lift a finger to help Gary Boulting to avoid capture neither would I, at present, assist to ensure that he was captured. As you know, I owe him, as it is sometimes simply and briefly said. With all that he might have done, he told me to walk away. I cannot risk all that the Superintendent and everyone including you, Carol and even myself have done, and are doing, by going to Boulting to say 'walk away —

122

now', but I wish to God he would do just that. He intimated that the contents of the van would be the last job for him. If greed prevents him from stopping now I will feel justified in doing what I know to be my duty. You are under no obligation to him but I do hope that you will be able to grant the favour to me, if not to him.'

'Surely, you know that. As you were speaking I was asking myself, were we to go on to Rouen, make the enquiries at La Salle et Cie., return to England by the night ferry and then report direct to Johnny. Is that about the time span you had in mind for this fellow?'

'You are what friends are all about. Gary Boulting could not in all conscience ask for a second longer.'

Tony went to the flight office for air taxis and made preliminary arrangements for us to be flown to Rouen. He made them in his name only, as a precaution in case of a tannoy call to go to the aircraft.

With a few exceptions the normal unit of flying instruction is one hour, so when G.D.1289 touched down and taxied to the hard standing fifty-five minutes after take off, leaving just sufficient time to reach the crew room and so complete normal training, was it just that or were we in at the end of a piece of split second timing by a former stunt flyer? Tony, needing no prompting from me, was already making his slow laborious way among the aircraft on the apron, looking the part of the enthusiast, examining with reverence and making detailed appraisal of each one. In due course he returned to the waiting room, to the seat beside me. With a dead-pan face and with controlled, slightly slower than usual speech, said: 'It is it. It has your moniker on it. It is the one.' The knowledge brought a feeling of relief and with relief a feeling of caution as I said: 'I think that is as far as we can take it, Tony. Gary Boulting is here and would recognise me in just half a glance. Too much gained to risk blowing it now, wouldn't you say?'

We entered the air taxi office and waited there until the aircraft was ready for take off. The flight took just thirty minutes and with the knowledge that the bank would close its doors at one o'clock we asked the pilot to be ready for our return flight at two.

Rue de Charenton was quite imposing, the premises 134/136 not nearly so. La Salle et Cie., however, seemed not to lack business if the number of staff, visible documentation and the size of the heavy iron safes could be taken as a guide. Their name on the windows of the floors above suggested that they occupied the whole premises.

Tony has remarkabe powers of imagination, allowing him to conduct a flowing conversation on matters not yet contemplated and hardly likely to be and so when we entered he acted for us both. Our difficulty with the French language was realised and overcome when we were shown to a desk at the back of the ground floor office, occupied by a pleasant looking brunette of about the middle twenties whose spoken English was a match for our own. The name block on the desk top introduced her as Suzanne Le Toure, to whom Tony said: 'We come over at least once every year, usually touring but on occasions taking an apartment for one month. We were wondering if there is an account into which we could make deposits sufficiently large that the interest would defray our expense while over here, but, er, without perhaps the necessity of our company cheque.'

She did not require him to labour further. A pleasant smile came to her face, brightening the look in her eyes, her voice considerate as she said: 'The taxes, they are a problem world-wide. You can deposit the French bank notes to whatever amount you decide. These last two days we have deposits of at least a million francs, that is exceptional but it happens so from time to time.'

'And you will first change the English bank notes?'

'Oh no monsieur. We are business bankers, we have no facility for the exchange but do not concern yourselves, there are many currency exchange dealers everywhere but for the large amounts we have Le Havre, Caen, Cherbourg and St Malo. Any place where there is ferry traffic or airports you will find them. The risk of robbery is very minute. I have only known of one, that at Cherbourg many months ago and then the money was not lost.'

'So we obtain francs, bring them to you, open an account and draw interest, when and how?'

'As you will monsieur, one month, three, six and if it remains for the full year there is an extra half of one per cent. We will pay here in cash, anywhere else in France and many places in Europe including Britain by our bankers order.' She looked at us enquiringly. We in turn, looked well satisfied with the information. Tony thanked her and expressed a hope that we might put it to effect on our next crossing.

At the end of our return flight we drove back to Cherbourg and our hotel.

Not as a fresh concession of a further twelve hours to Gary Boulting but we had become tired and decided against travelling on the night ferry to Portsmouth, choosing instead the mid-day sailing on the Sunday. The decision was a good one. We were well rested, the spell of fine weather had continued and as the majority of passengers were in either the cafeteria or restaurant sections we were comfortbly seated on deck bathed in sunshine.

I knew that Tony was itching to put to me a speculation upon which he had spent some time after we had retired to bed at the Coq d'Or. He had intimated that much to me at breakfast but although we had taken to laughing at our erstwhile spy novel posturing, we still did not risk becoming engrossed in conversation on that one particular subject while in enclosed areas. Gary Boulting's warning to me 'remember their strength is that everyone is watched', had made a deep impression on us both. But with only the sea spray to dodge away from we were very relaxed.

'This idea of mine, very little fact I am afraid, upon which I have tried to build a mountain of theory provides the link in the chain between Boulting and la Salle et Cie. And then the laundering of the notes, the proceeds of hijacks and hold ups is complete. What I could not rationalise was a host of people dashing into and out of bureaux de change with parcels of bank notes, the limit on which would probably be ten thousand francs or even less at each transaction.'

'Yes, that is the problem,' I interrupted, 'while Mlle. Le Toure, was speaking I visualised and rejected the picture of numbers of people in a procedure complicated by such numbers. Too many people and therefore too open to leaks on the one hand and extortion on the other for the Garlands and the rest to even contemplate.'

'Exactly. Now for my fact or facts: while we were waiting for the aircraft exchange, I noticed a small van pull up and remain parked near to Boulting's crew room. The driver remained seated behind the wheel. As Boulting and his pupil left their aircraft and went to the crew room, I nosied around the parked aircraft, as you know. As I made my way back to you, which would have been after an interval of about two minutes, I saw this same driver take four parachutes from his van and go with them into the crew room. Later, as we boarded our air-taxi he came out again and returned to his van, still with four parachutes. Now, I had no trouble in accepting him in my mind as the man from the parachute packing depot, department, firm, call it what you will, but in pre-sleep hours last night when I rejected masses of little people queueing up to change money, he came back very much into my reckoning.

Everyone would accept the sight of him as I had. He went only to and away from Boulting. I did not see him during our visit of the previous evening when James Boulting was there, although of course, that would not prove a thing either way. Now if you are with me thus far, Roger, I would like to develop conjecture into an acceptable picture of probability. But do shoot me down at any time if you think my reasoning to be a little up the creek.' I grinned at him my assurance that I most certainly would and he continued.

'My man with the van, shall I call him Joe, takes the parachutes to a safe place, removes the contents, from which he removes bundle bands with traceable markings. Then he drives to a place, or places, where he has built up a connection with the owners or operators. Joe will accept a low rate of exchange because he is not going to be asked questions. At the end of his run he will drive to La Salle et Cie. where someone nominated by Garland, Townsend or both will accept from him, say, one million francs in bank notes to be credited to accounts connected with the New Citizens League. The interest on those sums, and for that matter, any capital sum decided, to be paid through normal banking channels into League funds in England or to reward the likes of Masterson for a criminal job well done. So the cycle of crime and the laundering of its proceeds is complete. And Roger, a small but staggering thought could also be a true one. Joe could be an employee of a genuine parachute packing concern.'

'Food for thought and then some,' I commented. 'As theory there are no flaws but I suppose it will take a French counterpart of our Johnny Cousens to prove it. But in acknowledgement of your effort I would like to paraphrase, 'Oh what a tangled web we unravel when first, as detectives, abroad we travel.' Which left a grinning Tony holding his nose with left thumb and forefinger while making a chain-pulling motion with his right hand.

15

The certainty of fish and chips on the ferry seemed preferable to a possible snack on a not so probable dining car between Portsmouth and Waterloo and at the end of the meal it was time to slowly prepare for going ashore. Nothing to declare and would you believe that we were believed. The hired car was returned and they kindly drove us to the railway station. A good fast train is a rarity on a Sunday but we caught one and chose a taxi rather than the underground for the journey to Kennington. As we turned into the square we could see Tony's car at the kerb outside his house. So Carol was back but a police car was also there.

As we paid off the taxi Carol ran out saying: 'Tony darling we have been burgled.' Behind her came a young uniformed officer introducing himself as Constable Coombs.

'Mrs Fairchild has checked through and is satisfied that nothing has been taken, which puzzles me immensely, you have some quite valuable and easily disposed of items in there.'

By then we had entered the front door and were moving into the rooms on the ground floor. Everything moveable had been moved, every drawer emptied and the contents strewn on the floor; cupboards, including kitchen cabinets, had been clumsily disarranged. Tony was having difficulty in controlling his anger.

The constable said to him: 'Can you think of anyone who would commit an act of revenge or spite against you sir, for had theft been the motive, then with a car they could have cleaned you out.'

Tony answered: 'Yes, I agree, the fact that it is a weekend would have made it very, very easy. Quite a few of our neighbours, well Monday to Friday neighbours, are MPs. The square comes within the House of Commons bell as no doubt you know.'

'Yes, our number of patrols are kept up when they are in residence but at the weekend they and most other people in the square go off to the country.'

'Except the workers,' said Tony indicating himself, 'and to answer your question, no, I do not know of anyone who would indulge in vicious little games like this.' But I felt that he, like me, was beginning to think of just who they might be.

We had been upstairs to what was a similar picture of senseless activity and having returned to the ground floor, I collected items from the floor while Tony attempted to replace them to where they had originally been. Quite suddenly he stopped and seriously said: 'There is something missing Roger.'

'Is there? Anything valuable?'

'Not of itself but it is the all important copy of *Who Ever* magazine.' There was a long pause while he, Carol and I took in the importance of its loss. Constable Coombs said: 'Is it anything that should be included in my report?' We three appeared to be in hasty competition to tell him that it was not. Satisfied that he could once again think in terms of nothing missing, he left us.

Together we agreed that the break-in had been directed at Carol and Tony as a reprisal for their part in the weekend escapade and I said to Carol: 'They got near enough to know that Tony and I had left, it would seem.'

'They came very close and turned off just before I joined the motorway, it must have been a close run thing when you got clear away.'

Then Tony said: 'I am convinced in my mind that you should try to contact Johnny tonight, Roger. Carol and I have agreed with you that this intrusion is a message to us but finding the magazine leaves them in no doubt that you know everything about Helen Mandrake.'

'But it was found in your home, so I think I should correct what you have said: they are now aware that we all know about Helen, but I do agree that we should contact the Superintendent.' And I did so but by way of the ansaphone onto which I merely said: 'I am at Carol's'. and a call which Carol took which said 'Are you receiving visitors?' The answer 'Yes' brought him to us just twelve minutes later.

Greetings all round and then it was down to the business at hand. He listened very attentively to each of us and when either one, having commenced to say something, cancelled with: 'No, that is not important,' or the like, he would command it said with no more than 'It may be' or 'Let me be the judge of that'.

When we had finished he said: 'In co-operation with our French colleagues we shall move in on the Boultings and anyone connected with them. It is time for us to start pulling in the nets. I like your Joe the parachute man, Tony. I shall look forward to having a chat with him. Good observation and deduction, congratulations.' And with a grin, 'I must look to my laurels.' In a most elegant manner he had special thanks for Carol adding: 'Without your help these two could not have got started.'

Turning to me he said: 'Roger, I just have to take you out, haven't I. If they decide to get rough, you are number one. You know all about Helen Mandrake, we can leave the name as that for the present, and through her you have made yourself a real threat to Lord Garland and his son. Townsend is in no doubt and Masterson must keep reminding himself that you are the one who can name him

131

in connection with the van. Your hunt for the van's whereabouts led to Mills, and led you on to fly with Boulting. For how long, do you imagine, can the rest of them remain content that Boulting had been able to convince you that he was a flying instructor, nothing more? No, as I have said I must remove you from the scene. Now, what do you say to being arrested on a charge of your own choosing provided it is a matter on which I can have you held for one week, only one I do hope, or two at the most? I will guarantee restaurant prepared meals and Governor's quarters comfort and at the end, a statement acknowledging what a fine fellow you are.'

'Superintendent we have been this road before have we not, and as little as only four days ago. Believe me, I am no hero but you told me then that you still considered Helen would use any influence she had to shield me from harm. I agreed then and see no reason to change that opinion now.'

Johnny cut in quickly with:

'But it is a different ball game now. Then, they were all concerned with stopping you finding out about them, nothing more. Now it is imperative for them that they prevent you from halting their intention on the one hand and stop you from being instrumental in putting them behind bars on the other.'

'I really do appreciate all that you are offering to do,' I replied 'but I must take you back those four days. You said then that it was important I returned to my place of work, to my environment I think you said. That is as important now, is it not? And for the reasons you gave me then: the hope of avoiding the triggering of panic action. If I am not in my place in the morning I will have done more damage to the operation you head, than assistance. I am not personally an important factor either for or against them, but if I am not in my usual place they may

132

well assume that I have gone directly to you, the police, with the information they now know I possess which would, I suggest, bring about one of two panic actions. They would either rush to bring about their plan, causing irreparable damage to all that you, I and every decent Mr and Mrs Average hold dear, or they will run like hell.'

Johnny smiled as he said, 'If I could be sure they would choose the second alternative I would arrest you now and so prevent you being there in the morning.'

'That of course could bring about a temporary end to the threat they pose but I am sure it is not the solution you would seek in that you might not then discover and expose the top perpetrators. Only that could prevent the League functioning again but from an entirely new power base. And so Superintendent I would like to outline an alternative before you decide what should happen to me. I hasten to add that I will comply with your decision; I would be a fool not to.

'I propose that at the earliest opportunity I go to Helen, tell her what I have learned of her true identity, lay blame on Lord Garland and his son and assure her that I would think it a privilege to be regarded as her friend, confidant and champion. How does that strike the experienced police officer?'

A slight smile as he said, 'Yes, it might work, a bit over the top of course, Mr Nice Guy and all that jazz, but I am sure that is how she sees you. It might succeed and if it does, everything stays as of now for those few more, so very vital days. However I must insist on even tougher conditions from now on. No trips away from your place of work by day or usual haunts at other times; Use either Tony or Carol as the link to me. Use your messenger to get word to Tony. Remember all of these alternatives should you find even minor obstacles placed in the way of your freedom to make a telephone call before accepting an invitation to accompany Helen or answer a call to go alone to meet her. Get the message out first and you will not be alone. If, as you think, Helen is being used, she could well be used to lead you into danger. So a signal first, every time.' For a further fifteen minutes we all joined in light chat and banter before he left and I returned to my hotel for the first time in seven nights where, after the events of that period it seemed very ordinary, very normal.

Striding out across Lincoln's Inn Fields in soft morning sunlight, I knew that the proposed approach to Helen would succeed for the very reasons that my desire for her was undiminished and my intention to do all in my power to help her was as strong as ever.

No court duties had been allocated to me, so in official eyes the team of Mandrake and Diamond was still in being. I had no knowledge that she was in the building. After about an hour I rang her room and she answered. As is usual among colleagues I made the single word invitation 'Coffee?'

She accepted readily and not at all unkindly: 'Yes that will be splendid, the cafeteria at eleven?'

With thoughts of a crowded staff cafeteria and the words I had to say I suggested: 'The public restaurant will be rather nice.'

She agreed and was seated at a corner table when I entered.

As I spoke of what I had discovered she remained silent but her whole demeanour implied regret that I knew and the means by which I had learned. She did not mention the break-in at the Fairchilds and neither did I. But when I suggested possible influence or even pressure exerted by Lord Garland to enrol her help in the administration of the New Citizens League and all that we imagined that organisation to be, she threw back her head and burst into lengthy, mocking, high pitched laughter. Only when it had run its course and petered out did she say:

'Really Roger, surely you did not imagine that self opinionated windbag capable of initiating and controlling anything so complex. Why, he could not organise a garden party even with the help of the Vicar. No my friend, you will have to look further afield for your arch enemy, and that goes double for that precious son of his. A high point of success for that one would be to live on immoral earnings. I thought that you and I, in those first days, had accepted directly from his Lordship, his one concern, that nothing shall put at risk his social enhancing position which pays very nicely, to boot.'

Her stricture on the character of her husband led me to almost beg that she think of me as someone upon whom she could completely rely at all times and in any situation. A troubled look and she said: 'You are very sweet Roger. I once said that you were too young to die, or was it to live, I cannot remember. My high regard for you is often unbearable.' The steely self assurance returned as she scoffed: 'You are not one of life's winners but thank you for the coffee.' We parted at the doors to the restaurant and did not communicate again that day.

Just before five o'clock Tony came on the the internal with one of those cryptic messages, the like of which we had all adopted from Superintendent Johnny Cousens. 'Guildford, leaving at six, my car or yours.'

'Mine. With Carol?'

'Yes, she will be staying. I'll wait for you here.'

We arrived at Kennington to find that several items of luggage were standing in the hall ready for Tony and I to load into the car. To our expression of amazement Carol replied: 'You both supported the Superintendent in having me removed from my home and, as I am to go, I must have sufficient clothes to wear.' I turned to Tony saying: 'Humour her, it will be easier that way.' At which Carol

135

pulled a face before it became a broad grin, and we were all smiles as I drove away heading for Guildford.

Betty Fairchild took Carol off to be settled in very shortly after our arrival at the home of Tony's parents. It was very agreeble for me, an honorary member of the family, to observe the pleasure and pride in which she held her daughter-in-law. Tony and I followed Sir Brian into the lounge where in a party of four males, two were by now, very familiar faces: Chief Inspector George Dodds and of course, Johnny Cousens. We were very surprised to see them, Tony more so than I. His father had known that he would be travelling down with Carol and when he had asked that I be included we had assumed it would be to discuss with him our recent activities, in which Sir Brian would have a very special interest. Introduction of the others was brief, intentionally so I thought, just a name, no mention of rank if any, no hint of occupation or speciality.

Turning to us he said: 'You two young men are getting the red carpet treatment and rightly so. There has been a conference today here at my headquarters in Guildford, rather than in London, on the strategy to be used in the closing stages of this very odd business in which you have been involved. You will have no interest in its outcome mainly because we have no intention of revealing it.' There he paused to allow a warm reassuring smile to convey 'no offence intended' and continued:

'However the Home Secretary, who by the way regrets having been unable to stay long enough to meet with you again, has aked that we conduct this little briefing for you, not as a favour or as a reward but an entitlement after your contribution to our success to date. His words and mine and I venture to say those of all of us. Now that seems a bloody long winded way to say welcome so after a few moments in which to recharge our glasses, these men of fewer words but greater action will bring you up to date with both what we know and what we surmise.'

After the break it was Johnny who spoke first. 'I think you will be surprised at just how comprehensive a picture we can now present but first a minus. We do not, as yet, know the identity of the top man, never-the-less we are convinced that he is not far removed from the sphere of activity in which you have been engaged. You remember of course the Grainger tapes and will have wondered when you were going to hear them. The answer is that we now have, well Joe Longden has, edited the Grainger interviews and has included that on which we can rely with other tested material. Joe.'

I had already forgotten the name by which we had been introduced but Joe was not one who would immediately make a strong impression. Around five-ten, stocky, low on personality but I would guess, of high intellect.

He gave us brief and understandably scant details of the sources of information before continuing with: 'We know the names and in most cases full details of a large number of what I will call the middle order of management within the League. Grainger was enlisted into that category three years ago, 'the early days' he describes the period. There is apparently no promotion or movement to other areas of responsiblity once the initial allocation of duties has been made. The chain of command is of the conventional pyramid and each grade below has no recourse to whosoever has issued the instruction. In almost all cases he, or she, will not know the real identity of that person. This absurd form of secrecy has been accepted as necessary until they have made their bid for power. You will appreciate that once we make our move and interrogate those of whom we are aware, details of the rank and file will follow but the reverse is unlikely. In most cases the identity of even one member of a senior grade or grades will not be known and as a result the top echelon have felt secure in anonymity, that is until you two stumbled not just into the set up but at a high point within it. You have caused them to become quite a bit rattled. One can imagine heated arguments as to how to eliminate the danger to them that you have become. They have tried to warn you off, they have tried to frighten you away, but you are still very much there. Greater frustration will call for the involvement of very senior activists to deal with you. Many opinions will have been expressed but it will be the top man's decision. If it is to be an attempt to draw you into membership with an offer of money or positon then in our opinion, the offer will be made by number one himself. If force is contemplated and the decision to use it having been his, he is likely to be closely involved rather than trust knowledge of the act to others. So, by now you will have guessed the importance of your place in our efforts. We professionals do not as a rule, take kindly to amateur endeavour but you two are in a unique position. As we do not know them we cannot trail them but by keeping inconspicuous observation on you, we shall be right there when they decide to nibble. I understand that you will let the Superintendent know of any move by them, however trivial, capable of having that intention. You have forced them to bring their plans one year forward causing massive errors and bringing about their impending undoing. Mathews will tell what we have learned as to who they are, their hopes and aspirations.'

Up jumped an energetic little man of no more than five feet four, prematurely balding, but with a young face and eyes that indicated humour. He was the only one who had chosen to be standing whilst talking and with a broad grin said: 'With the rest of you seated it makes me feel good to tower over you. When Joe says who they are, it is a generalisation, names are meaningless but types are

138

interesting. The theme seems to be to radically change the existing pattern of public life. There are those who would, as they see it, make the change for the benefit of society as a whole, you know the type, ex service officers, not recent retirements but of the old school — 'What the hell is happening to the old country?' and those who want change because they have personally under-achieved. From the list I could name civil servants who made it to Principal but not Secretary, would-be Bank Managers who were stopped short as assistant. Barristers who were not offered Silk and their seniors having been passed over watched younger, and in their opinion, less gifted persons elevated to the bench. As to their hopes, I have seen much of the information circulated to members and I paraphrase. There have been so many years of vacuum at the political centre, they are optimistic that by exploiting the situation they may gain control at Westminster in one leap. The public regard for politicians is at an all time low. Ill mannered abuse and endless denigration of policies has produced dissatisfaction and despondency but no desire to turn to those prophets of doom and gloom for a solution. Hence a widening void which the League hope to fill. The general media, with an obsession for bad news have created an atmosphere from which the League hope to benefit with bright and constructive ideas. Aspirations: it would appear, from some of the writings, that the immediate objective in what they call Phase one, is not armed revolt. There are no arms and they do not seek head-on conflict. Their only force consists of a number of bully boys of whom Masterson is a prime example. With ever increasing membership and the campaign they intend to mount, they are confident of success in achieving power through the ballot box. Only then would their real aims become manifest. There is no mention at all of the possibility of failure and the notes refer to strong government of the kind that only they can offer.'

And Teddy closed with, 'Well there you are. It has all been heard before in so many countries.'

Chief Inspector Dodds passed on the news that Father Giles was dead, officially thought to be as a result of taking a large number of tablets but there were those in the Church who clung to the hope that it might still be recorded as a result of a heart attack. Tony remarked that his death would be the reason why Fergie had not returned to the courts that day, after his two week leave of absence, and reminded me that on our previous visit to Guildford I had said that if the League caused harm to Father Giles it would be a breaking point for Fergie.

Johnny said that a search of the disused Catholic Church in High Holborn, formally used extensively by the Citizens League, had not revealed information about them. He added that the demolition of the building must be imminent as the site had been surrounded by a high closed fence and he had seen the arrival of bulldozers there that morning.

As the meeting commenced to break up I remarked to Johnny my surprise at the comprehensive information possessed by Joe and Teddy, at which he repeated my statement to them, adding: 'Go on then, tell him how you do it?' A positive sparkle came into Teddy Mathews eyes as he said with a broad grin, 'In the furtherance of our investigations we have been members of the New Citizens League for about fourteen months.' Tony's dad said: 'If politics is the art of the possible, then policing is the art of recognising and countering the probable.'

It was time for the busy gentlemen to retire to their homes and Carol came in with mother-in-law to say farewell.

16

There was still no news of Fergie as I dialled his number for the third time and again drew a blank before going to the cafeteria at the coffee break. The day was proving to be the most uneventful since the amazing chapter of incidents had commenced in his room more than two weeks earlier. Helen and I had passed each other in the course of to and fro journeying from rooms, to courts, to offices and back, with no more than one spoken hello and a wave of the hand. During the afternoon, however, she had purposefully altered course and walked across the main hall to where Tony and I were in conversation.

She appeared to be bright and happy and almost immediately asked if I would accompany her to south London that evening to lend support to her bargaining attempt to purchase a second hand motor-car. I seized upon the opportunity saying that we might have dinner together afterwards, and I felt a flush of pleasure as she smilingly nodded acquiescence, saying that her car was in the car-park and would five-thirty be a good time to leave.

Tony said: 'That was natural and spontaneous, I cannot imagine that invitation to be the result of being used by others to way lay you, but where in south London are you going?'

'She didn't say and I didn't ask, I cannot treat her as though she were a criminal just because she is married to Garland's son.'

'I am sure that you are right but we must carry out Johnny's wishes. What is the index number of her car?'

'I don't know that either, I have not travelled in it

before.' I laughed at the thriller novel type conversation we were having. Good old Tony won in the end as he said: 'I shall ask the car-park attendant.'

Shortly after five-thirty I left with Helen in her smart little hatch back. With Helen in the driving seat I delighted in her company and waffled away on any topic that came into my head and it was with startled surprise I realised that the shallow forecourt onto which the car had stopped was that of the Crown, the pub on the opposite side of the road to Masterson's car showroom in Balham High Road. I could not think of anything more intelligent to say than 'Why here?'

She replied: 'Why not here? Do you know him?'

Still trying to regain full composure after the shock of arrival I answered: 'Who?'

'Charles Masterson,' and with her hand she indicated the showroom opposite. Feeling more capable of holding my own in the developing conversation I said:

'For a while there I thought that you were considering purchasing a car from a customer in a pub.'

'I am, Charles will be in the bar now.'

We entered the long bar. There was no mistaking him although I had not set eyes on him before. The suit, shirt, tie and shoes would equate with two months of my take home pay and the watch, its bracelet and the rings of solid gold, a similar amount. His florid somewhat flabby face and the thickness of his build were the result of over indulgence. He had, no doubt, been good looking in his leaner, hungrier years. There was no hesitation. He walked briskly through the bar to join us.

Helen said: 'Charlie Masterson this is Roger Diamond, a bright young star of the courts service.'

His hand and arm were outstretched, his smile a little forced as he said: 'The jewel in the crown, eh?'

As a riposte I fell back to one of my standards when

answering leg-pulls sparked by the name to which I was born — 'Well stone me!' at which Masterson burst into great guffaws of laughter and finally said:

'Stone me, I like it, I like it. Very appropriate, priceless, absolutely priceless.'

I turned to Helen saying: 'It surely wasn't that funny.' She looked more than a little embarrassed and quickly raised the subject of motor cars and they were still on that subject as Helen went with him to the other end of the bar to join yet another man. The three appeared to be in animated discussion, only occasionally glancing in my direction as I talked with the bar-man. As he turned to serve a customer I moved down to join Helen and the other two. I was not introduced to the newcomer and Helen did not demur as Masterson told him she was only showing off her boy friend, from which I assumed that no car deal had been struck. Masterson had lost interest in us and he left the bar a few minutes before we did.

As we came back into central London we decided on the l'Opera restaurant just off the Strand for the meal. It was the first time since Bournemouth that we had devoted time to one another. I was thrilled and pleased to note that I was not alone in my feeling of relaxed happiness. At one stage during the meal I briefly referred to the conflicting moods of ecstacy and sadness experienced at Bournemouth and that it had emphasised an impression I had formed of one so very tempted to snatch at happiness and yet almost immediately to firmly and bitterly reject the notion as having no part in a life that she saw for herself, adding:

'I hope that you will not be offended if I say that I find you quite an enigma.' Lovely smile but the troubled look fleetingly returned to her eyes as she said:

'No, of course I do not mind because it is true. I experience all of the joy, the fun and the vitality of a young woman. I love to dance, sing and to cry a little, to compete and to achieve. To be sexually attracted to that certain man who walks into one's life as you did. They all add to something approaching seventh heaven for almost all except the committed, would-be achiever. Please understand when I say that to lightly brush any or all of those pleasurable senses can only be to the good in one's life but dwell with them and they become as lead weights to someone who feels a calling, a destiny.'

'Oh come off it Helen. Destiny, that is a bit over the top,' my voice registering dismay and disappointment.

'Is it? Could not the feelings of prime ministers when entering number ten be so described, or those of a scientist embarking on a project that will bring benefit to mankind, or a young churchman dreaming that his dedication may bring peace and justice to all.'

'Yes, of course, but what do you feel to be your role, your destiny, Helen?.

'Feel to be my role! I knew my destiny from the moment I accepted who I was. I knew the road, I knew the milestones, I knew my goal. Nothing in life was more certain. Then along came Roger Diamond. Your very being a guarantee of safety and security to the woman in me. Of love and warmth, a fireside glow in winter with kids in their beds above. Of comfortable mediocrity. I told you only yesterday, my regard for you is unbearable when set against that which I must do. The undoubted effect which in a short while you have made upon me is expendable, my destiny, as we choose to call it, is not.'

It was all so final and in the depression it brought me I could not attempt to make a case for myself against it. I very lamely asked: 'And what of Bertram Garland in your future?'

'A stepping stone now, nothing more,' she replied.

I looked again at a young couple seated at a nearby table. I had noticed them earlier, the way one might give attention to a feeling of being observed. I thought that I must know them and then it dawned on me, the young man had been seated at the rear of the bar of the Crown public house earlier and his companion had been waiting, seated in a car outside. I had been secretly chaperoned all evening. I had an almost irresistable desire to thank them for a job so very well done but the night was still young and instinct dictated that I should not reveal their presence even to the lovely person who still meant so very much to me.

The evening had too soon sped away and Helen insisted that she drive me to my hotel which is no more than a pleasant walk away from the restaurant. As I climbed the three steps to the hotel entrance I noticed the car which had pulled up not more than fifteen yards behind Helen's and did not leave until she had gone. I turned into the hotel with a clear thought: 'Johnny Cousens, you do not make idle and empty promises.'

The following morning as I sat at my desk engaged with the allocation of cases to court, some not to commence before a whole year ahead, I found myself wondering where I might be at the end of such a period and what, if anything, would be my association with Helen. Of course I wholeheartedly applauded her determination to be a top achiever, who could do otherwise, but I failed to see why it had to be to the exclusion of a normal healthy relationship of the kind I was so eager to offer.

I had hardly put thoughts of her from my mind when it was she who burst into my room, beside herself with anguish:

'Roger, Roger we must get to the old All Saints church. Mr Ferguson is there and will be killed.'

'Now Helen, take it slowly. What is Mr Ferguson doing there and who told you about it?'

'He has gone to the belfry to make a protest. He left a note. But, Roger, we must go now or it will be too late and he will be killed.'

I took her by the shoulders and shook her and with the strongest voice of command I possess said: 'I want to know and I want to know now, what note and from where and why to you?' She was now much calmer and quite lucid.

'Mr Ferguson left a note on his desk, Mrs Mason found it because the door to his room had been left open. She phoned through to me.'

'Why you?' seemed to express my puzzlement.

'I really don't know except perhaps that I had called her just two minutes earlier to ask if she had news of his intended date of return.'

'Where is the note now?'

'On his desk. I haven't handled things at all well have I? But do let's hurry.' We ran along the corridors until we reached Fergie's room. Mrs Mason was not to be seen but the door was wide open and on the desk a note printed in biro.

I SHALL STAY IN THE BELFRY OF THE OLD ALL SAINTS UNTIL I HAVE BEEN ARRESTED. THEN I WILL PUBLICLY DENOUNCE THE MURDERERS OF FATHER GILES.

IAN FERGUSON.

'But he does not refer to danger,' I asserted.

'He does not know that the church is to be demolished today. If they do not see him he will be killed,' she replied.

'You stay here and await Mrs Mason's return, she may have more news. I will ring through to this extension when I have found him.' An arrangement which she readily accepted.

Outside the main entrance I hailed a taxi and asked for the old church in High Holborn, not as a result of what I had been told or the words I had read but because that note had not been made by Fergie. Whoever penned the note had not risked handwriting for fear that I would notice the writing as not that of Fergie. So they had printed it, not realising that Fergie's printing was more distinctive than his writing ever was. It was always his habit to make a tiny flourish to the beginning and end of each and every letter. He printed as he had in the so called index number clue which had led Tony and I to Masterson's show rooms and workshop.

Before the taxi came to a halt I could see the sectional close fencing which entirely surrounded the site, a necessary precaution against injury whilst the demoliton was in progress. The driver had pulled up beside a hinged double door section, large enough to allow vehicles to be driven on and off the site. As I paid off the cabby, however, I found that a large padlock was securely in place.

Choosing an anti-clockwise direction I made my way until I came to a narrow unsecured door which gave easily to my push. The area appeared to be deserted as I walked around the inside of the fence until I could see at the far end two huge vehicles. One was a broad mechanical shovel capable of scooping up fallen rubble and effortlessly raising it to deposit the contents directly into a lorry. The other, positioned closer to the walls of the tower, resembled a massive army tank, in that mobility was obtained by way of huge caterpillar tracks. The superstructure consisted of an operating cab together with a long, strong metal arm, capable of controlled movement through all directions, from the end of which, suspended by a thick iron chain, hung a massive ball of metal, or stone and metal combined. Operated from the cab the arm would swing the heavy weight until it crashed against a wall, reducing it to rubble in a fraction of the time required by a whole gang of workmen with picks and shovels. Wishing not to attract attention to myself, I retraced some steps and entered by a door space at the side of the building. What must have been a stout and heavy door had already been removed, as had all of the pews and the altar.

As I moved through the large empty space of what had been the nave I called loudly: 'Fergie this is Roger Diamond, if you hear me call out.' There was no reply and I called again, as loud as my voice was capable: 'Fergie are you alright?' I had by then, come to the enclosed space at the bottom of the tower, reserved for bellringers and around which an old oak staircase spiralled to the top. I slowly climbed the stairs pausing on two occasions to call again: 'Fergie are you there?'

At the top, the stairs led onto a bare, wooden floored platform of about two metres wide extending around all four walls of the belfry tower, enclosed on one side by the walls and restricted on the other by a wooden post and rail fence. I walked along one side and as I turned the corner I saw Fergie huddled on the floor close to the wall. I rushed to his side. He was quite dead. He had been murdered. There was a bullet hole at the back of his head just below the skull. Looking closely I could see that the point of exit had been the socket of his right eye. It was apparent that at the time of the terrible deed he must have been restrained either manually or secured with ropes or, as I preferred to think for dear Fergie's sake, while he was unconscious. It was then that I saw the weapon lying in the narrow floor space between his body and the wall. It was a .22 Barretta revolver with mother of pearl handle of the type I had seen pointed towards me in Fergie's room such a short while before. Suddenly the need to vomit was irresistible and as I half slouched over the fence rail, the noise it made as it met the floor below emphasised not only the emptiness of a church dismantled but also the desolation I felt at the brutal removal of the life of a friend.

To breathe fresher, sweeter air I went over to one of the large gaps in the nearby wall, one of the many that allow the sound of the bells to reach out to the four corners of the parish. Looking down to the demolisher, as I thought the huge mechanical vehicle must surely be named, I saw two men in the cab, one at the controls the other immediately behind him in a position consistent with holding a gun at the other's back. Both wore safety helmets and protection goggles but for me there was no mistaking the one behind the man at the controls, it was Charles Masterson. The realisation of the trap into which I had so tamely walked numbed my senses and yet thoughts raced through my mind. There would be two bodies and a gun to be found later among the debris: Fergie the victim, myself the assumed murderer. The previous evening Helen had taken me to Balham, not to help purchase a car but to be identified to Masterson in the furtherance of the dastardly act he was now about to carry out.

The need to get below and away galvanised me into action. It would be as though deserting Fergie but he was beyond my help, beyond the help of anyone except his God. As I began to move away there was the most terrifying crash and the boards below my feet shuddered as though trembling. The huge iron ball had struck a corner of the tower walling but the platform was still intact and my bewildered mind found relief in such thoughts as what a poor shot! A mere glancing blow! Poor shot indeed! It was a remarkably good one as I realised when I reached the point where the platform met the stairs and I looked down. A gaping hole in the wall at rightangles to the one beside me and the whole section of stairway previously attached to it now lay broken and shattered on the floor below. There was no escape.

I went back and looked over the parapet at Masterson, who upon seeing me gesticulated indicating that for him it was a moment of success. He knew there could be no escape, he had no need to hurry, his warped mind could savour his moment of triumph. He was one who would enjoy killing. I now realised the meaning of his hilarious outburst at the pub when I had said: 'Well stone me'. More thoughts raced through my head. Was not one supposed to review a lifetime on such an occasion. I thought of the conflicting attitudes Helen held toward life and love and people. It could only be that there were two Helens. It must surely be so. Could the explanation be the onset of a form of schizophrenia? A wild guess perhaps, from a non-medical man but I was in a crazy situation. I thought too of my miserable failure to carry out Johnny Cousens' explicit instruction to contact either him or Tony in such a situation. I had done neither. I was alone.

Moving across to the rail fence I looked up to where the bells were still in place, to the hinged blocks to each that caused them to swing and ring, and the ropes that tilted the blocks. The ropes. They were there, they were in place. Very old now of course, and only ever intended to pull the weight of a bell but some bells could be quite heavy. To contact the nearest would involve a leap outward coupled with a fall of some six feet before being in a position to grab at the rope. I could not expect one to hold me but hoped that it might check my fall whilst I gathered one or more of the others to me. Grabbing at bell ropes, grasping at straws! If I stayed I was going to die anyway. I climbed and sat upon the rail of the fence, facing towards the ropes. Making the one leap that counted I clung with hands and feet to the rope, causing the bell to sound one resonant clang before coming stationary to a side-on position. As it did so the consequent jerk caused the rope to begin slipping through my hands until with my foot, I was able to swing twist the portion of rope immediately below me twice around the calf of my leg. Releasing my right hand I gathered in two more ropes and using both hands twisted all three together as I made my descent to the floor below.

Being over anxious to get swiftly to safety I stumbled and fell full length onto the rubble already fallen. I staggered up and ran out into the nave just as a second blow brought most of the belfry tower tumbling to the ground.

A young man was coming towards me and having reached me made an attempt at dusting me down with his hands saying 'Are you alright, Sir? Superintendent Cousens will never forgive me for allowing you to get into this state.'

A moment later a radiantly relieved Tony came dashing up, so full of explanation that could hardly wait to be told. It was Mrs Mason who had told him of the note and under his barrage of questions Helen revealed that it was I who had set off to join Fergie. Jubilation turned so quickly to distress as I told him of the fate that had come upon our close friend.

As he and the young police officer were escorting me to the gate in the fence there was a burst of sporadic gunfire, so close that we all three flung ourselves to the ground and as he did so the policeman produced in his hand a .38 revolver. There being no more gunfire he continued to usher us from the site. I got the impression that his personal responsibility was our welfare and not to get involved in a gun fight other than to protect us.

Outside we saw Johnny Cousens standing on the roof of a police car with a hand microphone to his mouth, directing what he later called 'This piddling little operation.' He was in a light hearted mood by then and congratulated me on my 'Hollywood act', which put everything into a perspective with which I could cope and diffused the remaining tension within me. But he was more serious when telling us that the gunfire was brought about by Masterson who, having first tried a hopeless dash to escape, arrogantly and stupidly turned and fired at his pursuers. From the marksmen officers he had sustained three bullet wounds, one of which gave cause for concern as there had been extensive haemorrhaging.

Johnny quietly informed Tony and I that arrests were being made in various parts of the country and would include Helen Mandrake.

17

The next few days were strenuous and somewhat chaotic. Masterson had died of his wounds and had surprised everyone with an act of honourable decency before death overtook him. He told doctors and nurses that my escape to live from that which he had planned and believed would be certain death, and he, the would be killer, about to die, could only be the will of the Almighty. He had asked that a priest be with him at the end. The very long statement he made to the police entirely corroborated that made by Helen. She had played a full part in getting both Fergie and I to the belfry but only in the belief that Masterson was to, as he himself put it, give us one hell of a scare and so get the two of us off their backs. He added that Helen had always been the voice against violence in the furtherance of their campaign.

Carol had returned to Kennington to be with Tony and we were all together in the court when Helen was formally charged with what I thought the clerk read to be conspiracy to rob. The words, even had I heard them correctly, meant very little as I looked upon the distressed young woman in the dock. The death of Fergie had had a worsening effect on her already troubled mind and her physical appearance was that of a wilted flower when compared with the radiant personality we had all known. Superintendent Cousens told the Magistrate that he would not oppose bail pending the remand hearing, that I was a suitable person to stand as surety, that accommodation had been arranged for her at a nursing home and that Helen undertook to attend as an outpatient, the clinic of an eminent psychiatrist. Bail was granted on those conditions and Carol, Tony and I drove down with her to the nursing home at Marlow with its view of one of the lovely stretches of the Thames.

Johnny Cousens had intimated that no charges more serious than the one I had heard read out would be preferred as Masterson's statement had eliminated her from any complicity in the death of Fergie. He was of the opinion that two years imprisonment might be the maximum and, in his own words 'When the doctors have had their say the court may decide that a non-custodial sentence will be appropriate'.

So the future was full of hope. At the clinic they were confident that with modern drugs Helen could look forward to a quiet normal life, perhaps without some of the sparkle but also without most of the depression. And for me, wasn't that the sort of life I wanted to share with her. What the heck was a two year wait anyhow!

After two whole weeks the psychiatrist said, that for me to take her on an outing would be conducive to Helen's well being. I was overjoyed. For me to participate in her rehabilitation would be a wonderful memory well into that future we could now plan together. Carol prepared the picnic, Tony selected the wines and I set off with their blessing for a very special date with Helen. I drove first to Runnymede and she listened intently as I said that to most of us it meant more than just a beauty spot because of its historic association with rights and freedom which led eventually to the mother of parliaments. We British, a nation of very independent individualists, could all, although alas to varying degrees, have a big say in our own affairs.

She perked up and showing an increasing amount of interest said: 'But there must be order to hold the line between liberal freedom and anarchy.' I saw the look that had come to her eyes and decided to move, not just from the subject but also from the place.

A short distance further on, we came to an idyllic spot for the picnic with a car parking space close by. It was good to see Helen taking charge of the spread and we agreed that Carol had done us proud. The delicious meal, the setting, the soft spring weather but most of all the noticeable, however slight, improvement in Helen after only two weeks and I experienced contentment for the first time since that day when more than church walls collapsed.

I supposed that it must have been our talk at Runnymede that prompted Helen to say: 'You British were my grandfather's big mistake. He did not underestimate you and always wanted to take you along with him. He wrote that to have been allied would have brought a new order to Europe and thus influenced the world.' She must have seen the look of incredulity on my face as I asked:'

'Your grandfather?'

'Yes, the one person responsible for who I am and for my burden of destiny. My mother was the daughter of Eva Braun and my fabulously wonderful grandpa Adolf Hitler.'

My jaw dropped a little. Any tiny desire to even smile I suppressed in deference to the heartfelt sincerity with which she had spoken the words.

I gathered a few items of picnic-ware together as I anxiously said: 'Shall we go back to the home and watch television, Pet.'

She was becoming excitable and said: 'That's right, imprison that with which you cannot contend.'

I remembered advice from the staff at the clinic, to go along with and naturally respond to her moods of both high and low. I am not a psychiatrist and could not know any more than anyone else whether perhaps a truth in what she had said was responsible for her condition or if fantasy could be so strong as to have lived within her not for just days but for years. I wanted to believe her and said: 'Tell me about it Helen, about your destiny.'

She gave an enquiring look into my face before speaking. 'She was a baby girl when taken from the Chancellery in early nineteen forty-five and placed in the care of family friends who took her with them to Argentina. Grandpa used three thick note books in which to write for her a book about his aims and also his desire that she take up the cause for him. In his belief that she would do so he had written instructions as to how she should make it come about. She, poor soul, saw his defeat as a mark of failure, not only in war but in all that he did and tried to do. Even her marriage to my father, Godfried Mandorff, failed to instill interest in the history of her parents or indeed in the fortunes of Germany. When I became old enough she gave the book to me to read, not as a book of learning but to interest me sufficiently to afford her moments of peace and quiet. I read it then and regularly in the years thereafter. It became my second bible and through it I came to know him as though he were alive, particularly throughout my formative and impressionable years.'

I was quite spellbound, not only by what she said but also the convincing manner in which she said it.

'And was that the reason you came to England?' I asked.

'Of course. It was an early instruction in his own handwriting, to correct his mistake by bringing together Britain and Germany, not in just a pact but by means of a binding union. Only then, he wrote, would war be eliminated. And I would have succeeded, Roger, if you had not come blundering in. I told Lord Garland that I must be put in a position where I could counter every move that the inquisitive Mr Diamond made and convince him that he probably imagined the little he already knew.

'But I had not allowed for the impossible to happen. I fell hopelessly in love with you almost on sight. You were the only rival Grandpa ever had and between the two of

156

you I faltered, my judgment became unsure and often flawed. My dilemma has been that the demanding claims you and grandpa make upon me are incapable of compromise. To turn to you and the wonderful life we could have together would be a betrayal of the unswerving steadfastness I had promised to the Grandpa his book has created for me. Alternatively, to carry out his wishes I would have to lose you.' She pointed to midstream where a portion of branch from a tree having fallen into the water, floated on by. 'Now I am like that piece of wood, drifting aimlessly yet fearful of sinking.'

'Helen you must see that together we will do much to bring about his desire, not perhaps by political pressure with all of its pitfalls but by real honest effort through the arts and cultural societies. We will help to make every town here a twin to one over there. You cannot blame yourself for failing to keep a promise to a ghost.' She shivered, not at the word but because a cloud had temporarily denied us sunshine. I asked if she would like her cardigan from the car, she nodded and I walked the short distance to get it.

Returning, I was seized by the sight of Helen wading out into the river and laying herself down in the water. Like the log, she drifted, just for a moment before sinking below the surface. As I ran I was screaming out, first to her and then to anyone who would hear me. I ran directly into the river making for where I had last seen her and where I thought she might be. When the water became deep I swam below the surface trying to see her but I had disturbed mud at the bottom making a sighting impossible. I had seen no one on the bank and yet I was yelling to everyone in the world to look and point her out to me, that I might save her. Reason seemed to be leaving me as I flailed with arms and legs in the hope of striking against the body I could not see.

I was then aware of strong arms restraining me and of

being forcibly dragged to the bank, still yelling that Helen must be saved, that I was alright. It was two men who held me and two more were coming out of the water further along the bank. In answer to my pleading they told me they had found her but that she was not responding to artificial respiration.

I wanted to run to her but my legs and arms would make no movement. Were it not for the firm grip my rescuers still held I would have sunk to the ground. I tried to beg them to take me to her but words would not come.

It was then I started crying and knew that I would never stop. The convulsive sobbing, the only movement my body would allow and that I was unable to control.

EPILOGUE

Walking through lovely gardens in autumn sunshine I know that at last a tranquil and potentially happy future has been restored to me. Dr Ruskin, who would have saved Helen and made her well, has instead done those things for me. I was overjoyed at the eventual release from the confines of the wheelchair followed by relief from the cumbersomeness of crutches and it is now three days since I threw away the walking stick. You are right, of course, I have been a temporary resident at Dingly Dell, the nursing home to which we brought Helen that long, long while ago. Tomorrow I am to be discharged and will be going to stay with Tony's parents at Merrow for two weeks before fully returning to the world outside. I look forward to the visit and I know that Betty and Brian will love having their other son, the adopted one, to stay awhile.

Helen has her rightful place in my memory; that of a truly remarkable person and the most beautiful woman I have known or ever will know. No more need for my mind to tussle with the conflict of an overwhelming obsession to bring her back and simultaneously reject and repel the traumatic events that had surrounded her. I now regularly walk to the far side of the gardens and enjoy the delightful view along the Thames. It is so very peaceful once again.

Maybe the world will never know whether or not she was who she claimed to be. Personally I believe her. But it matters not. In her own right she was a fabulous administrator, an ingenious forward planner, a supreme controller and most especially, fascinating to behold.

Nurse Melanie Blake has made life here so very tolerable. She has been an almost constant companion, at the possible expense of her other duties I fear, but she seems to have

Dr Ruskin's approbation. Carol and Tony indulge in playing match-makers with invitations to make a four to almost every event in the calendar and Carol's whispered utterances of 'third time lucky' could hardly go unnoticed. I think it is perhaps that she is a little broody. She has informed Tony that he is to become a father in the spring.

Superintendent Cousens has visited often, he is only a short distance away, on a course at the police college. Sir Brian tips him to be next or next but one to become head of a police force and is prepared to wager that Johnny will be the youngest ever Chief Constable.

Every effort has been and is being made to play down the whole episode concerning the New Citizens League in order not to afford them any of the destabilising effect they strenuously sought and planned before the arrests.

Every penny stolen by way of hijack and bank raid was recovered due to the sums having been handled exclusively by La Salle et Cie. Only the earned interest was lost, having been used in the furtherances of the League. Apparently it had always been Helen's intention that the illegally acquired sums would be restored once the aims of the League had met with success. The rift between herself and Masterson was a result of his avaricious desire to get control of the millions held by La Salle et Cie.

All members of the League other than the few at the top table, as Gary Boulting described them, were unaware of the criminal actions employed to raise funds and were dealt with for minor offences at local Magistrates courts where the imposition of a fine was considered to be appropriate.

Brian Garland was separately arrested for his own offence of being the owner and operator of an unpleasantly sleazy porn club in Soho. As the recruitment of youngsters was part of his vile trade the Judge had no hesitation in sentencing him to two years imprisonment.

Dealing with Lord Garland, and with an over-riding

desire to deny to the League the publicity of a fashionable show trial, adroit diplomacy was employed. He is to be the Governor of Gibraltar. But what he will know and the public will not is that the guards around him will be keeping him from us and not us from him. If he had a trade union his representative might tell him that he has a job for life. He has a life sentence! He will never return to Britain.

Have you noticed that when shocking things happen anywhere around the world people tend to say it would never happen here. But my thoughts will reflect on the truly amazing events that did intrude once upon a life!